SILVER HEELS

Michelle Lynn

Published 2020

Printed in the United States of America
Print ISBN: 978-1-951490-50-8
Ebook ISBN: 978-1-951490-51-5

Canoe Tree Press
4697 Main Street
Manchester, VT 05255

www.CanoeTreePress.com

The poem "The Musical Story of Art" is dedicated to the power that our soul has in listening to the healing sounds of nature, so painting a new picture of hope is right outside our door. The music of nature is one of most influential sounds we can listen to in shaping our destiny. The sounds of nature open up the imagination to the beautiful symphony of "I am..."

I also want to dedicate this book to the spiritual world, and my beloved sister, Laurie Beth, who had the mind of a creative artist and continues in spirit to motivate me everyday on my journey to chasing my *Hollywood Dreams*.

THE MUSICAL STORY OF ART

The Ocean crashed,
The water flowed,
The flowers whispered
Good-byes, as
the morning dew
Touched Her flesh with
Purity to
Paint a
Portrait
Her voice couldn't
sing, but only her
Hands could
Compose, and
Her heart could
feel,
Note by note,
Her hands began to
underscore the
greyest area,
beat by beat,
She began to hear
The melody of
Her gift to paint

TABLE OF CONTENTS

CHARACTERS IN HOLLYWOOD DREAMS

SKYLAR: HOLLYWOOD DREAMER, EXOTIC DANCER "SOLEIL," AND NICKNAMED THE DANCE QUEEN AT SILVER LIGHTS.

ANASTASIA: REAL ESTATE COLLEAGUE AND ENTERTAINER AND NICKNAMED "HAPPY ENDING DANCER."

REDMOND: ASSISTANT MANAGER AT SILVER LIGHTS. REFERRED TO AS "COUNTRYMAN" AND NICKNAMED "HAWK" IN SILVER LIGHTS.

JOHN MARINO: NYC WALL STREET EXECUTIVE. WORKS RIGHT UNDER THE OWNER OF SAPPHIRE INVESTMENTS AND CAUGHT IN FEUD.

PHILLIP DELFONTE: WALL STREET EXECUTIVE THAT WORKS FOR SAPPHIRE INVESTMENTS. KNOWN AS "THE BLOW JOB KING."

CASSANDRA DELFONTE: PHIL'S SOON-TO-BE EX-WIFE. HIGH POWERED CONSULTANT WHO HAD AN AFFAIR WITH BROOKS KENNEDY FROM ONYX EQUITIES, HER HUSBAND'S RIVAL FIRM.

CRAIG PETERS: WALL STREET EXECUTIVE WHO WORKS WITH JOHN MARINO AND FOR SAPPHIRE INVESTMENTS.

CHARLES MARZIANO: BILLIONAIRE AND HEDGE FUND OWNER OF SAPPHIRE INVESTMENTS AND FUND IN NYC. CANDIDATE FOR MAYOR 2020 AND NICKNAMED "THE BEAST OF WALL STREET."

CAMDEN ROBERTS: STOCK ANALYST AND ALLY TO JOHN MARINO WITH INSIDER INFORMATION.

MICHAEL DONAHUE: SENIOR CHAMPAGNE HOST. SECRETLY WORKS FOR BROOKS KENNEDY'S FIRM ONYX EQUITIES.

BROOKS KENNEDY: SOCIALITE AND OWNER OF ONYX EQUITIES.

GIUSEPPE BAR BACK: AT SILVER LIGHTS AND WORKS FOR EDDIE MAGGIO.

EDDIE MAGGIO: OWNER AT NEW YORK CITY SECURITY CONFIDENTIAL.

ARTURO: OWNER OF NEW YORK CITY SALON, ARTURO'S. STYLES THE MAYOR'S WIFE'S HAIR AND THE EXOTIC DANCERS. KNOWN AS "THE HAIR GOD."

CINDY: ARTURO'S ASSISTANT.

CLAIRE MAHONEY: WIFE OF NEW YORK CITY MAYOR AND RUNS IN HIGH SOCIETY.

THOMAS MAHONEY: NEW YORK CITY MAYOR WHO HAD AN AFFAIR WITH AMBER RAY.

BARBIE: EXOTIC DANCER AT PENTHOUSE, UNDERCOVER SPY FOR SILVER LIGHTS AND REDMOND'S GIRLFRIEND

TONY MURANO: HEAD OF SILVER LIGHTS AND PARTNER AT DIAMOND HOSPITALITY. KNOWN AS "THE LION KING."

VICTORIA MARINO: TONY'S GIRLFRIEND AND JOHN MARINO'S SISTER.

ROSE HIGHWATER: NICKNAMED "THE GOSSIP QUEEN." SOCIALITE AND BROOK'S KENNEDY NEW GIRLFRIEND. FORMER EDITOR OF THE NEW YORK POST.

DJ PAULY: SILVER LIGHTS DJ

LOLA: PREMIERE ENTERTAINER AT SILVER LIGHTS AND MICHAEL DONAHUE'S LOVER. KNOWN AS "THE QUEEN BEE."

FRANKIE MARTINEZ: ASSISTANT CHAMPAGNE HOST AT SILVER LIGHTS AND RELATIVE TO FRANK DELUCCA.

STEVEN BANKS: CEO OF GEMSTONE HOSPITALITY AND VENTURES.

BROOKS KENNEDY: POLITICAL AND SOCIALITE HEIR. OWNS ONYX EQUITIES.

AMBER RAY: NEW YORK CITY'S BIGGEST PORN STAR AND SILVER LIGHTS BIGGEST MARKETING TOOL. HAS AN AFFAIR WITH THE MAYOR.

LEVI SANCHEZ: FORMER MODEL, PORN STAR AND RELATIVE TO CARLOS SANCHEZ.

LUCINDA: BARTENDER AT SILVER LIGHTS.

BRIANNA: EXOTIC DANCER AT SILVER LIGHTS AND ASPIRING SINGER.

KAITLYNN: DANCER AT SILVER LIGHTS, INTERNET MODEL, AND NURSING STUDENT.

WHITMORE REYNOLDS: PRESIDENT OF THE NEW YORK STOCK EXCHANGE.

CHRIS BANKS: AGENT AT GRAPHITE ENTERTAINMENT AND STEVEN BANKS' COUSIN.

CHRIS BANKS, SR.: PRESIDENT OF GRAPHITE ENTERTAINMENT.

SUSAN BANKS: ENTERTAINMENT AGENT WHO WORKS AT GRAPHITE ENTERTAINMENT AND SISTER TO CHRIS BANKS.

LOUIS MAZARATI: OWNER OF EMERALD INVESTMENTS AND FINANCIER IN CHARGE OF THE LARGEST PONZI SCHEME.

GABRIELLA MARINO: JOHN MARINO'S WIFE.

PIERRE LUCA: FRENCH SOCIALITE, BILLIONAIRE, OWNER OF RANDALL PHARMACEUTICALS, AND "DARK KNIGHT" TO SKYLAR.

ANGELICA MARCELLO: FORMER DANCER AT SILVER LIGHTS WHO RECEIVES SILVER INVITATION FROM PIERRE LUCA. MARRIED TO CARLOS SANCHEZ.

CARLOS SANCHEZ: HEAD OF THE LAS VEGAS MOB.

STEFANO MARCELLO: PENTHOUSE OWNER AND AFFILIATED WITH THE MOB.

ANGELO BIANCHI: PENTHOUSE OWNER AND AFFILIATED WITH THE MOB.

RON COLUMBO: HEAD CAPO FOR THE MARZIANOS, AND HEAD OF THE DRUG CARTEL RUN AT PENTHOUSE.

NICHOLAS GRECO, SR.: NICKNAMED "THE SHARK." SERVING A PRISON SENTENCE. FAMILY LINEAGE USED TO BE THE HEAD OF THE MAFIA UNTIL THE MARZIANOS CAME INTO POWER.

NICHOLAS GRECO, JR.: SON OF NICHOLAS SR.

TOMMY D: MOBSTER AND CAPO FOR BOTH MOB FAMILIES.

DOMINICK SANTORINI: MOBSTER AND CAPO FOR BOTH MOB FAMILIES.

ROBERT FELDER: CROOKED COP THAT WORKED WITH THE GRECO FAMILY.

VINNY MARCELLO: GANGSTER WHO OWNS THE LARGEST SANITATION BUSINESS IN BROOKLYN.

FRANCO MATTHEWS: STOCKBROKER FROM 1980s. RUNNING A FINANCIAL SCAM IN PARTNER WITH THE GRECOS.

DONALD SINGER: CO-FOUNDER OF EMERALD INVESTMENTS AND TONY'S FRIEND.

GREG SAUNDERS: FORMER FBI AGENT WHO SENT THE GRECO FAMILY TO PRISON. HAS MOB AFFILIATIONS WITH THE MARZIANOS.

ALFREDO MARZIANO: "GODFATHER" OF THE ENTIRE MOB FAMILY, BROTHER TO LUIGI MARZIANO.

LUIGI MARZIANO: HEADS THE MARZIANO FAMILY WITH HIS BROTHER LUIGI.

RODGER MATTHEWS: EXECUTIVE AT EMERALD INVESTMENTS.

LUKE MATTHEWS: CHAMPAGNE HOST AT PENTHOUSE AND AFFILIATED WITH THE DRUG CARTEL.

TERRY BIANCHI: COUNCILMAN AND THOMAS MAHONEY'S RIGHT WINGMAN. COUSIN TO ANGELO BIANCHI.

TED CONNORS: FINANCIAL CONTROLLER FOR ONYX EQUITIES.

BLAKE STEVENS: FINANCIAL CONTROLLER AND COUNSEL FOR DIAMOND HOSPITALITY, SILVER LIGHTS ENTERPRISE.

GRANT LAWRENCE: CEO OF VITAL PHARMACEUTICALS AND CLOSE FRIEND TO BROOKS KENNEDY.

JOEY HENDERSON: VP AT DATA INTEGRATIONS AND VENDOR WHO WORKS WITH SILVER LIGHTS.

TRAVIS KEYS: VICE PRESIDENT OF AMERICAN FREEDOM AND VENDOR WHO WORKS WITH SILVER LIGHTS.

FRANK PIAZZA: FBI LEAD ON THE LOUIS MAZARATI CASE.

PIERCE MAHONEY: TONY'S ATTORNEY FOR THE LOUIS MAZARATI CASE AND RELATIVE OF THE MAYOR.

JAKE RYAN: SOCIAL MEDIA CELEBRITY AND INFLUENCER.

FRANK DELUCCA: SILENT INVESTOR OF GEMSTONE HOSPITALITY. ASSOCIATE OF THE MOB FAMILY, OWNER OF CAPITAL BUILDING AND FRANKIE MARTINEZ'S RELATIVE.

MICHAEL KENNEDY: BUSINESS TYCOON AND BROTHER TO BROOKS KENNEDY. WORKS FOR ONYX EQUITIES.

CAMDEN ROBERTS: FORMER VP AT PRECISION INSTRUMENTS AND STOCK ANALYST.

MARC MELVIN: PRESIDENT OF GRAMERCY REAL ESTATE.

SALVATORE MARZIANO: NICKNAMED "THE SNAKE" AND ASSOCIATE OF THE LARGEST CRIME FAMILY.

KATHERINE MAY: SOUTHERN BELLE AND THE BEAST OF WALL STREET'S FOURTH WIFE.

FRANCESCA FERRARI: SENIOR DIRECTOR FOR SUNSHINE ALTERNATIVE ENERGY INC. POSSIBLY RELATED TO THE LUXURY CAR FAMILY, THE FERRARIS

MELINDA MASTERS: WIFE OF GOVERNOR TYLER MASTERS AND CHARLES MARZIANO'S LONG-TIME MISTRESS.

TYLER MASTERS: NEW YORK GOVERNOR.

HENRY ROMANO: PRESIDENT OF SUNSHINE ALTERNATIVE ENERGY INC. HAS MOB AFFILIATIONS.

GRACE DONAHUE: FORMER MODEL AND MICHAEL DONAHUE'S WIFE.

BRAD ROSSDALE: NEW YORK CITY'S TOP PRIVATE INVESTIGATOR.

TREY: ANASTASIA'S BOYFRIEND.

INTRODUCTION

The life of becoming a "star" in the world of *Silver Lights* has taken Skylar Lynn's character, "Soleil" to another level of dreams. After finishing her first screenplay, *City of Dreams*, Skylar Lynn, an aspiring Hollywood star, is caught in the web of her second feature, *Hollywood Dreams*, and there is no turning back. *Hollywood Dreams* has skipped past the different dreams, different scenes and one feature story portrayed in *Silver Lights*, and fast-forwarded to a jam-packed, explosive drama with Wall Street scandals, organized crime, and a forbidden love affair.

The Silver Heels give Skylar faith in her award-winning role as the exotic dancer, "Soleil" that her second screenplay, *Hollywood Dreams* may eventually be more than a *Page Six* story. For Skylar, *The Silver Heels*, like *The Silver Lights*, radiate in her scenes, protecting her character and guiding her to chase her Hollywood Dreams amidst a bleak forecast. It is through the supernatural powers of *The Silver Heels* that she is able to prevail in her new role as an exotic dancer, still capturing her authentic voice amongst the scenes of organized crime, Wall Street scandals, and champagne-fueled rooms of "sex, drugs, and rock n' roll."

CHAPTER 1
SMOKY DAYS

Smoky days were looming ahead for the cast of *Hollywood Dreams*. The thick smoke started to spread around the new setting of *Hollywood Dreams*, creating a darker storyline for Wall Street's biggest rivals, Sapphire Investments and Onyx Equities. These days, Sapphire Investments was lagging far behind Onyx Equities. However, about two months ago, this wasn't the case, it was the complete opposite. Sapphire Investments was killing it on the stock exchange as Onyx Equities was hanging on by a thread. In the world of Wall Street, when high-powered deals are at stake, anything can happen, even a bomb going off!

The chances of a bomb being set off on Wall Street in Skylar's second feature, *Hollywood Dreams*, was likely when two rivalry firms were fighting tooth and nail for the number one spot on the exchange.

About two months ago, Sapphire Investments and Onyx equities were playing out this scenario, fighting each other hard for acquiring one of the biggest technology accounts, Precision Instruments. Sapphire investments went as far as trying to get illegal insider information from Precision Instruments, which ended up blowing up in its face. This unexpected bomb set off in Sapphire Investments' face detailed an exact recorded conversation taking place between John Marino, former managing director at Sapphire Investments and his associate, Phillip Delfonte about using insider information to acquire Precision Instruments.

John's exact words, "Do not repeat this to anyone. The kicker is, he has an insider person from the company named Camden Roberts giving him confidential information that their stock is going to double with the launch of their new software platform, Galaxy." This set off a series of explosions that Michael Donahue, Senior Champagne Host at Silver Lights, happened to play with. Michael Donahue, a former white-collar criminal, loved playing with fire, because it made him lots of money. He played with this exact fire by taking the hard evidence of the recorded conversation and selling it for $600,000, in a deal that Brooks Kennedy couldn't pass up. The deal would give Michael back his life of luxury with a series of deposits that would make his bank account $600,0000 richer.

While Michael was on top of the world and getting back into the life of luxury, Charles Marziano, known as "the Beast of Wall Street," and his firm, Sapphire Investments, began to shatter to pieces. The destruction and aftermath had burnt not just the company, but its big shot executive, John Marino's character in every way. His life was getting smoky going from a charming executive to a miserable associate in days. Charles Marziano was left with no choice but to forfeit Precision Instruments based on the former. To make matters worse, not only did Sapphire investments have to sign a compete clause around Onyx Equities' top technology customers, but their corporate bank account dwindled, leaving "the Beast of

Wall Street" fifteen million dollars broke to keep his company from being audited by the Securities Exchange.

Meanwhile, John Marino's life was quickly spinning out of control. A former addict, he started using again, bathroom binges of cocaine, morning whiskey shots in the office and late-night rendezvous with high-end hookers. He became paranoid about trusting anyone in the world of high-end mergers and acquisitions. He learned never to discuss confidential information in public places, or anywhere he could be set up. His life at home mirrored a daytime drama. His marriage was on the rocks and his former penthouse downgraded to a modest two-bed room apartment on New York City's Upper East Side. From the moment John woke up, he became consumed each day about finding the person that ratted him out.

However, in the game of cat and mouse, there was a slim chance that John would be able to see through the smoke on a good day in the production set of *Hollywood Dreams*, and catch Michael, a highly trained criminal. Michael was fearless in his actions, because he was confident there were no witnesses at the time, but little did Michael know that someone was watching him set up hidden cameras. That someone happened to be a bar back named Giuseppe whom Michael failed to notice. Giuseppe clocked in early like he always did to prep the bar for the evening, as Michael Donahue's hired third party, Eddie Maggio began to set up hidden cameras.

ACT I, SCENE 1
MONEY TALKS

FADE IN

Seven weeks earlier, late afternoon

EXT: New York Streets

Giuseppe, a young hard-working Italian from Brooklyn, was hired by Tony Murano to help with bar operations. At the time of the installation of the hidden cameras, bar back Giuseppe checks in early to prep the bar for the night. He notices a technician working, Eddie Maggio, owner of NYC Security Confidential. It's odd that Eddie is working without Tony's supervision, placing hidden cameras throughout the VIP rooms. Giuseppe's curiosity piques as he sees Eddie install cameras in odd places, so when Eddie leaves after the job is finished, Giuseppe chases him down the street to find out more.

DIALOGUE

GUS: Hey, Hey. (*shouts*)

EDDIE MAGGIO: (*turns his head*) What's going on?

GUS: You were just in *Silver Lights*.

EDDIE MAGGIO: Whoa, and who may I have the privilege of talking to?

GUS: I'm Giuseppe, but call me Gus. I work at the club you were just at.

EDDIE MAGGIO: Oh, *Silver Lights*. I was just finishing a work order that Tony requested.

GUS: Usually everything for security is set up when Tony is on site.

Eddie Maggio, a close friend of Michael's, and business contact of Tony's, has been doing security at Silver Lights for the past few years. However, this security job was not run through Tony. Eddie is a middle-aged, short Italian man who owns NYC Security Confidential, a high-end surveillance company catering to all the clubs and restaurants in New York City. He is trained to handle these situations.

EDDIE MAGGIO: You're very smart. I should hire you! Tony gave Michael permission and I have Tony's contact information (*showing his phone*). We go back to the streets of Brooklyn.

GUS: What part of Brooklyn?

EDDIE MAGGIO: Bensonhurst. I'm guessing you're Italian, and that you have been to Francesca's Bakery and Rosalina's. My favorites are the crème filled cannolis at Francesca's and the angel hair marinara from Rosalina's.

The moment Gus hears the name, Rosalina's Restaurant, his tone changes and his interrogative questions stop. This guy Eddie is the real deal, and he pretty much slaps Gus in the face to back off! He makes it clear with his word associations of Rosalina's and Francesca's that he is an associate, someone who does business frequently with the mob. These are mob-run places where organized crime meetings are held, and characters just know when they hear those names, danger is right around the corner.

GUS: My favorite is the vodka penne from Rosalina's. The tiramisu from Francesca's was a big hit with my family's pizzeria before it got shut down. We used to order 50 miniature tiramisu cakes each week to deliver with pizzas.

EDDIE MAGGIO: Sorry about that. Here is my business card (*hands him the business card*). I think I can help you get your pizza place back. I'm actually looking for someone young and sharp like yourself to help with my workload. I'm not sure exactly what you pocket at the club, but if you are looking to make an easy three hundred dollars a week or possibly more, give me a call. You never know, maybe I can become a silent investor in helping your family get their pizzeria back.

GUS: That would be amazing. I just have to check my schedule at the club, so it won't interfere.

EDDIE MAGGIO: Call me and we will work something out. (*his phone is ringing*) I have to take this.

Eddie Maggio goes in the direction of the number 6 train back to his midtown west office, while Giuseppe goes back to the club to clean up the bar. The extra three hundred dollars a week will help his father's cause in restoring their pizzeria back to original state. A few weeks ago, an anonymous John Doe set a fire and it happened past operating hours. The store was completely destroyed, with insurance only covering half the costs. The cops said based on the matches and gasoline they found near the pizzeria, the fire was not an accident and it was a crime of arson. Unfortunately, since there were no cameras or witnesses, their insurance coverage had clauses that limited their liability coverage in restoring the restaurant back to its original state.

FADE OUT

"Money Talks, Bullshit walks," and this expression was no stranger in the feature screenplay, *Hollywood Dreams*. For Gus and his working-class family, the money and future investment in their pizzeria that Eddie would offer Gus, in exchange for silence, would keep Michael Donahue's ass out of trouble a little bit longer.

However, Michael Donahue at any scene still faced the possibility of being caught, because Gus would have even more hard evidence the longer he worked for Eddie Maggio. He would inherit full access to all security records of every hospitality establishment in New York City, including the establishments run by New York City's biggest crime family, the Marzianos. If Gus was to rat Michael out too early, the fate of Skylar's second screenplay, *Hollywood Dreams* could be ruined.

CHAPTER 2
BLONDE AMBITION

Skylar Lynn learned that in the playground of exotic entertainment, nothing was off limits. Every night at Silver Lights, there were cocaine binges, threesomes, blow jobs, money laundering, illegal gambling and Wall Street scams taking place in the champagne rooms. If that wasn't enough for a hot drama, there were major *Page Six* stories igniting everywhere, especially in the hair salon!

The hair salon was a place where drama was captured at every angle. Anyone who stepped foot in the salon had the possibility to get trapped in the burning drama throughout *Hollywood Dreams*.

Skylar came to the hair salon not only to escape drama, but to take her role up a notch by becoming an eye-catching blonde with lots of ambition. The person to accomplish this would be "the Hair God of Instagram," Arturo.

ACT I, SCENE 2
THE SAME DRAMA, DIFFERENT DAY

FADE IN

INT: Arturo's Salon

Week 7 after Skylar's audition

Arturo's is a popular New York city salon among the entertainers. Arturo, the founder, a sexy metrosexual guy from Brazil, just loves surrounding himself with beautiful woman. He is a big shot hairdresser in Manhattan.

His business first got recognized after the story spread that he was doing porn star, Amber Ray's hair, and the mayor's righteous wife, Claire Mahoney, at the same time. Rumors were floating around that Thomas Mahoney had a one-night stand with Amber Ray. At the time, Thomas failed to check the background of the escort agency, as there were hidden cameras placed everywhere in the hotel room where he slept with Amber Ray, costing him hundreds of thousands of dollars in legal fees.

Skylar met Arturo during her fifth week at Silver Lights, when he was doing a dancer's hair in the dressing room as way to promote his services. He handed her a business card and said, "Darling, I'm going to make your hair Instagram-worthy." He was obsessed with his social media portfolio and to him, Silver Lights was the perfect opportunity to blow up his reputation. The one thing Arturo failed to overlook when deciding to work at Silver Lights was the inherent drama that came with each blow out and style. There was so much drama doing the hair of exotic entertainers that each blowout, cut or color entailed a dirtier secret than the next, possibly jeopardizing his Instagram reputation as the #hairgod.

Today, he is doing Anastasia's hair. She is a dancer at Silver Lights and a real estate colleague to Skylar.

DIALOGUE

ARTURO: How is everything?

ANASTASIA: Nothing has changed. The same drama, different day.

ARTURO: With Bri and Lola?

ANASTASIA: Yes, but there is more. You will never guess who got hired.

ARTURO: Rose Highwater?

ANASTASIA: Seriously, did you have anything to drink today?

ARTURO: Yes, I did, I had a Tequila sunrise.

ANASTASIA: Still, a Tequila sunrise should awaken your senses to the big picture. Rose Highwater has enough money to buy this building and Silver Lights. I could just see the headline now on *Page Six*. "Socialite Becomes a Stripper?" (*chuckles*)

ARTURO: I can beat story with this headline: "Mayor Does Porn Star."

ANASTASIA: Dish it.

ARTURO: Just promise me, Ana, you cannot repeat this to anyone.

ANASTASIA: I promise.

ARTURO: Claire Mahoney, the mayor's wife, was getting her hair done about six months ago when she confessed to me that her husband secretly paid both press and attorneys to cover up his one-night stand with Amber Ray. The night they hooked up, there were hidden cameras placed all over their hotel room.

ANASTASIA: How much did he have to fork over?

ARTURO: Enough to keep this porn out of the spotlight. Now, speaking of Rose Highwater, she is a donor for the mayor's 2020 campaign. Claire went out of her way to thank Rose by setting her up with Wall Street's hottest playboy, Brooks Kennedy.

ANASTASIA: They are dating? (*upset*)

ARTURO: I'm not sure dating is the correct term, but shagging is!

ANASTASIA: It's not going to last. He goes for anything that gives him a hard-on, especially when he is fucked up on cocaine.

ARTURO: I recall you saying he is good with his tongue? (*giggles*)

ANASTASIA: Shh… Keep it down.

ARTURO: No one is listening.

There are few other people in the salon getting their hair done.

ARTURO: Who else did they hire that is stirring up drama?

ANASTASIA: Remember that girl, Skylar Lynn, from my real estate office?

ARTURO: *The Sex and the City* writer and Hollywood wannabe.

ANASTASIA: Well, you will never believe this, but she is a stripper at Silver Lights and her stage name is "Soleil." To make matters worse, she is working with the Queen Bee, Lola.

Arturo remembers talking to Skylar a few weeks ago and giving her a business card. He freezes up, realizing Skylar could pop in any second.

ARTURO: (*playing stupid*) What does she look like?

Anastasia takes out her phone and shows him a picture of Skylar, smiling in her real estate picture. Arturo looks at her with the expression he knows exactly who she is and as a matter of fact, of all people, she is scheduled to walk in any minute.

ARTURO: I talked to her a few weeks ago in the dressing room and she is coming in today to go blonder.

ANASTASIA: Well, please don't share anything I just mentioned.

ARTURO: My lips are sealed. Everything you say is between us. Anyways I thought you liked her.

ANASTASIA: I don't dislike her.

Right when she says that, Skylar walks through the door with an energy drink in one hand and her navy handbag in another. She is rocking skinny denim with a fitted crème top and wedge-like sneakers. She looks a bit surprised to see Anastasia getting her hair done. She waves and heads toward Anastasia and Arturo.

SKYLAR: Hi, nice to see you. *(gives her a hug)* We just keep running into each other.

ANASTASIA: First the club, and now my hairdresser. *(jokingly)*

Skylar takes a seat next to Anastasia

SKYLAR: I'm not following you, I swear. Arturo asked me to be a promo model for Instagram.

ANASTASIA: I'm joking. By the way, how is the club?

SKYLAR: I am really digging it, but still trying to figure out those crazy Wall Street boys.

ANASTASIA: They are easy, just wait until deal with the Marzianos.

SKYLAR: The Marzianos?

ARTURO: Lesson number one, if you are going to be a stripper in New York City, then you have to become familiar with the Marzianos. They practically run all strip clubs and restaurants in New York and in some areas, they run the police.

ANASTASIA: They also own half of Brooklyn real estate. You know the Capital Building deal that Marc is trying to get his hands on?

SKYLAR: The 8-million-dollar deal that is pretty much up in the air?

ANASTASIA: Yes. The investor and owner is Frankie Delucca. He is a long-time associate of the Marziano family and he is smooth Frankie Martinez's relative.

SKYLAR: Is it his uncle? Does that mean Frankie is in the mob too?

ANASTASIA: No, Sky, don't be ridiculous. Frankie isn't part of the mob. He says he is far removed from that world. He mentioned they are distant cousins on his mom's side. I'm warning you right now, some of them have a poisonous tongue, and when you get too close it stings.

Skylar looks surprised, but her curiosity is piqued, making her ask questions.

SKYLAR: So I need to be ready to play with fire when they come in? How can I spot them? In the movies, many of the leaders wear rings on their pinkies.

ANASTASIA: That's one way to tell, but the second way is that they have a *Sopranos*-type personality. You know the mob drama on HBO in early 2000 that ran for six seasons?

SKYLAR: Of course. So you're saying I should look for a clone of Tony Sopranos?

ANASTASIA: Not exactly a clone physically, but personality-wise, yes. Look at all the classic mobster traits of a Tony Soprano. Most of them dress in nice suits and are impeccably groomed. Also the head guy lets his wingman do all the talking in the public, but behind doors it's a different story. Frankie Martinez is the guy from the club that deals with them directly the moment they walk in. He takes them to the Howard Stern champagne room, and then grabs them the flavor of the day—from the top shelf champagne to the most popular of entertainers. Most of them prefer blondes but some prefer an exotic flavor. Oh, and Michael usually hangs out with them when he is on shift and your new best friend, the Queen Bee, typically does rooms with most of the associates.

SKYLAR: Really which ones?

ANASTASIA: Last I heard, she did a room with Salvatore the Snake.

SKYLAR: Sounds scary. Why do they call him the Snake?

ANASTASIA: He is sneaky motherfucker. You just never know when he will show up to the club, and he better like you in the champagne room otherwise all hell breaks loose for Redmond and Michael. Word on the street is if you mess with any of his businesses laundering money, he will strike like a snake out of nowhere!

SKYLAR: He sounds interesting. He could be what my second feature screenplay, Hollywood Dreams needs.

ARTURO: Honey, he is dangerous. I'm sure there are other characters that are easier to deal with for your second feature.

SKYLAR: Easy isn't necessarily the best choice when it comes to writing a feature drama. I believe a character like Tony Soprano—one that looks like your neighbor from the outside, but from the inside is a violent sociopath waiting to explode—will give my feature an edge.

ARTURO: I think the edge your feature needs is you becoming a blonde bombshell. (*runs his hands through her hair*)

Skylar is so excited about running into these Tony Sopranos type characters Anastasia is describing. The material she could capture in a group champagne room with these guys could be the riveting dialogue her feature needs to make it to the top. The anticipation starts to build around the dangerous characters from New York City's most notorious crime family, the Marzianos, setting up her feature, Hollywood Dreams, for a possible movie deal.

SKYLAR: I'm ready to take on Silver Lights as a blonde bombshell.

ARTURO: I'm going to make you more than just a blonde bombshell. You are going to be one smoking hot goddess! (*he runs his hands through her hair*) My hands are magic, everything I touch turns into gold. I'm going to make you a golden fantasy when a customer comes in the club. (*getting a text which signals with a sound*)

Arturo receives a text from Claire Mahoney about her appointment for her hair style for a high-end event the night of Saturday March 14th. He looks down and the text reads, "I am bringing two other people with me next week so block off the afternoon." Whenever she texts, Arturo drops everything to accommodate her. She is responsible for Arturo's reputation as "the Hair God." She gave him his first break as a celebrity client and invested thousands of dollars in his salon for advertising.

SKYLAR: Is everything ok?

ARTURO: Oh yes, I just have to head over to the client book and check my schedule. A high-profile client of mine who runs in the circle of New York City politics needs me all day Saturday the 14th of March. Ana, I will finish with you when I come back. I need about five more minutes with you before Cindy will wash the color off. Sky, I'm going to mix the color to start your transformation.

Arturo heads over to the front where he makes the changes to the schedule, while Anastasia and Skylar talk before he heads back.

ANASTASIA: How was last night at the club? Did any big spenders come in?

SKYLAR: It was slow. No one worth mentioning except Brooks Kennedy. He came through the back door and went straight back into the Howard Stern champagne room.

ANASTASIA: So, what are his chances he will be in tonight?

SKYLAR: Slim.

ANASTASIA: Well, he has a socialite girlfriend now, so maybe that's why he is going in on Mondays.

SKYLAR: Who?

ANASTASIA: Oops, I wasn't supposed to say that. Just forget this conversation.

SKYLAR: He may come to our annual masquerade party so don't give up hope.

ANASTASIA: I'm actually hoping he brings his brother Michael so I can close two deals in the champagne room by shoving my tits in his face. (*chuckles*)

SKYLAR: Just make sure it's not being recorded.

ANASTASIA: What happens in Silver Lights stays in Silver Lights. When Tequila is involved, Michael Kennedy becomes a willing party animal!

Arturo comes back from the front desk after taking a phone call and talking with his young blonde assistant Cindy. He hears the words "Party Animal"

ARTURO: Did I hear the words "party animal"? Who might that be?

ANASTASIA: We were just referring to Michael Kennedy, Brooks Kennedy's brother. I would be surprised if you have heard of him.

ARTURO: I read about him six weeks ago on *Page Six*, regarding his firm acquiring Precision Instruments, and I know they are having a celebration gala at the Waldorf Hotel. I have Claire Mahoney coming in the day of their celebration party, less than two weeks from now, to get her hair done.

SKYLAR: The Waldorf is a hotel where only fairytales happen. It's the place to hobnob with the rich and famous.

ARTURO: This event is high profile and invite only.

ANASTASIA: We have the Silver Lights annual masquerade party a week from this Thursday and there will be plenty of high rollers.

Skylar starts to let her imagination run wild for a few seconds, envisioning herself dressed like a modern-day Cinderella, attending this exclusive party, dressed to the tens at the Waldorf. Hypothetically, if this storyline was to take place, her second feature could take a dramatic turn, changing the dialogue and dynamics of her staring role as an exotic dancer. Just like that, Cindy's voice wakes Skylar out of her daydream.

CINDY: I have an appointment in 30 minutes. Let's get her washed.

ARTURO: After you remove the foils, do two washes and put the toner on for ten minutes, then rinse with cool water. When you start to blow her out, I will come back to check the color.

CINDY: Follow me and I will get your foils off and washed. (*she looks at Anastasia*)

Anastasia gets up

ANASTASIA: Sky, don't forget about the marketing campaign for the Capital Building. Frank Delucca is one of the owners in the deal, so you may have a chance to meet him with Marc.

SKYLAR: I will set some time in my schedule next week to work on it.

ARTURO: Sky, I'm ready to make you one hell of a blonde bomb-shell with my godly hands, and it's going to be Instagram-worthy. Do you have an account? (*excited*)

SKYLAR: I do, and it's called onceuponazen.

ARTURO: Interesting handle. Sounds like a fairytale.

SKYLAR: It's a fairytale in progress.

ARTURO: My dear, your fairytale is just starting with the magic of my hands and will only get better from here on.

Skylar smiles after hearing "will only get better from here on." Arturo gets to work on Skylar's highlights as Anastasia finishes up at the shampoo station. Her toner cools the warm and brassy highlights. Anastasia leaves super happy with his work. Her hair has baby highlights of cool blond in the front and her shadow root has some lowlights of blonde mixed with her brown roots. She is rocking cool blonde highlights with long layers. Arturo snaps the back of her hair for his Instagram handle, hashtagging it #hairgodofinstagram, then he gets back to work on Skylar.

Three hours pass. Arturo is finishing the last few touches on Skylar's hair as her former honey brown hair with subtle highlights becomes a full blonde bombshell with hues of warmer blonde highlights in the back and cooler blonde highlights in the front, still leaving a shadow root at the top. He finishes the blowout, and Skylar is on cloud nine with how good she looks. The makeover is just what her new role needs to begin her fairytale with the world's hottest French bachelor and billionaire, Pierre Luca.

SKYLAR: I'm speechless. I can't believe this is me. *(looking in the mirror)*

ARTURO: Just say "I'm too sexy for this Instagram" as I snap your hair. *(Arturo grabs his cell phone)*

Arturo takes pictures of her hair color, and then tags her Instagram with his account. Just right then Skylar is getting a text message alert from Redmond, assistant manager of Silver Lights, saying, "We need dancers tonight for the early shift. Please come in before the club opens."

Skylar's heart literally skips a beat while reading his text. From the moment she met Redmond in her first feature, City of Dreams, her character knew the countryman's soul from somewhere else. He was indeed her twin flame from another lifetime, and shortly, in the fourth act of Hollywood Dreams, both her and Redmond experienced their flashback from the 1920s, explaining their former relationship.

The thought of her and Redmond getting it on, after hours in the champagne room, is still a fantasy of hers. She dreams of him throwing her against the office wall, assertively grabbing her face and tugging her hair, kissing her neck and then deeply French kissing her. Then taking his masculine hands near her ass and ripping off her G-string, gently caressing her in all the right spots that get her so excited and wet, she wants to have sex all night. Just by being in his presence, she can feel the way he kisses and imagine the way he would insert himself in her.

From the way he looks to his charms, Redmond was born to be a good lover. Flirting comes naturally to him, as does the way he makes other dancers feel protected. He must be a rock star in the bedroom, the way he caters to a woman's needs. No wonder Barbie, his girlfriend, sticks around amidst the cheating rumors. Skylar can see in Redmond's aura the way he would make love to her if they ever hooked up. She envisions how he would first kiss her soft and sensual, then get a rhythm going that would be more intense and passionate, stroking her G spot with his hands and then his perfect cock. She's never imagined sexual intimacy could feel so real without sleeping with someone, but she knows strongly in her heart and soul that she and Redmond were former lovers in another lifetime, possibly man and wife, mistress or lover. She can't identify the exact nature of their relationship. She's never experienced a fantasy that feels so real, with strong sexual desires that make her warm and tingly inside. She'll just have to wait for the second half of Hollywood Dreams, in the final act, to make sense of their twin flame connection and the life they had in the 1920s.

The text is beeping again, and it snaps her out her fantasy with the countryman. She needs to get home, get ready for the night, and get to the club. She texts Redmond back immediately and says she will be there shortly. Although Skylar is somewhat obsessed with their soul connection, this would fade away once she hears the French accent, catching her off guard with the words, "C'est un plasir de vous rencontrer. Tu es belle." (Translation: Pleasure to meet you. You are beautiful)

FADE OUT

CHAPTER 3
THE BOMBSHELL

It was little over a week until the masquerade ball, and there were whispers circulating around the club about what celebrities would be in attendance. Seven weeks had passed since Skylar's start date, and bombshell after bombshell was exploding at the premiere gentleman's club, Silver Lights. From the latest bombshell of porn star Amber Ray having sex with Redmond, to Redmond's bombshell girlfriend, Ava Marie (known by her stage name, Barbie) working both as a dancer and spy at Penthouse, to the biggest bombshell of all: the Louis Mazarati scandal making its way to the front entrance of Silver Lights. And of course, you couldn't forget the bombshell of Wall Street's dirtiest secret that would skyrocket *Hollywood Dreams*.

Both Sapphire Investments and Onyx Equities had tons of skeletons in their closet, including the major feuds brewing up over customers, their concealed violations with the New York Stock Exchange, and the list was getting longer by the minute. Their dirty laundry list entailed counts of black mailing, financial fraud, tax evasion, money laundering and a possible conspiracy theory with the president of New York Stock Exchange, Whitmore Reynolds, and the New York City government.

Thomas Mahoney, mayor of New York City, was backed by many of the elite Wall Street firms. His voice was powerful in both the political and economic landscape of New York City. When the markets were on the up, businesses were burgeoning and the international currency rate of the dollar was 1.5 up the Euro, making New York City a favorable place for many European investors.

Mahoney, a well-known politician and a former Wall Street tycoon, was part of a conspiracy with the American government that influenced consumer spending on a worldwide scale, making New York City a top contender for international investors. Mahoney's motives were for political gains. He had money that afforded him multiple estates, unlimited spending, private jets, and a mass fortune of five hundred million dollars. His political career, however, was lacking, and far behind his mass fortune he had accumulated. He knew his chances for the 2025 New York State Senate were slim. He also envisioned himself working one day as a cabinet member for the President, but it seemed too far off. During his short time as mayor, business was on the up, but his power was non-existent as he dreamt to be a bigger political figure.

If he succeeded in his dreams of rising up the political ranks, the drama rising in *Hollywood Dreams* would spill out. His strong ties to New York City's largest crime family, the Marzianos, and the New York Stock Exchange's President, Whitmore Reynolds, could either make or break Mahoney's political career, assuming his own dirty laundry wouldn't come out.

The question was, how would Thomas Mahoney go about establishing a reputation in national politics as a voice to be heard. Would his new political Campaign for a "Brighter Apple" be enough for him to garner attention, or would he have to appeal to an international market to give him the extra push he needed to be in the forefront of national politics? There were so many questions left unanswered, and it would be in the last act of *Hollywood Dreams* that Thomas Mahoney would have the opportunity to move into the forefront of national politics.

Mahoney would have his chance three months from now, in June 2020 on election day, to prove to New Yorkers how he was the better choice than the Beast of Wall Street. With markets being unpredictable, and feuding rivalries at an all time high, the Beast of Wall Street's mind was far removed from his campaign these days. If Charles Marziano wanted to do something right for once and all in the feature, Hollywood Dreams, it would be to win the seat of mayor of New York City. The victory would create a monopoly on Wall Street for their firm, and the feud between Onyx Equities would come to a halt. The best part would be his newfound power with the city, and his close relations with state and national officials would make his reputation bigger than he could ever imagine.

Although he had his hands full trying to regain the number one spot on the exchange, he would soon realize the solution to his declining position on Wall Street would be the victory over Thomas Mahoney. In the seedy world of the Beast of Wall Street, this meant being a vicious animal in taking down his prey. Would his animal instincts kick in so he could go to extremes in being the "the Beast" he is and destroy his prey, Thomas Mahoney? He would first turn to Brad Rossdale, New York's number one private investigator, to track all of the mayor's donors, financial dealings and secure records Marziano he could discover a bombshell that would blow up Hollywood Dreams into a blockbuster.

CHAPTER 4
SILVER HEELS

The Silver Heels, just like *the Silver Lights* in Skylar's first feature, *City of Dreams*, gave Skylar the momentum to dance through the darkest scenes, pushing her character to the edge each night as she faced the fiery drama of sex, drugs, money laundering and volatile dialogue. In *City of Dreams*, it was the special powers of *the Silver Lights* that guided Skylar out of darkness and into her staring role as an exotic dancer. In *Hollywood Dreams*, *the Silver Heels* radiated when Skylar was either in danger, dancing on stage or near someone important, especially French playboy and billionaire, Pierre Luca.

One thing was certain: Tuesdays were tequila nights at Silver Lights, and there was no escaping the dangerous drama fueling this tequila kind of night, as one intoxicated Wall Street executive, John Marino, made his usual rounds.

ACT I, SCENE 3
A TEQUILA KIND OF NIGHT

FADE IN

INT: BAR AREA AT SILVER LIGHTS

John comes in searching for Lola, but is disappointed when he realizes she is not there. Skylar notices John's appearance even more this time: his muscular frame, masculine jaw line, perfectly groomed goatee and manicured hands. His unforgettable dimples match his perfect teeth. The one thing that resonates is the way John called her "Baby" in their last encounter in City of Dreams.

Skylar sits at the bar watching another dancer from afar, as John comes up to her. He is intoxicated and he glances at Skylar for a minute and can't recall when he met her. The blonde hair and sexy image completely throw him off. He turns his attention toward the bartender, Lucinda, to get a drink.

DIALOGUE

LUCINDA: Hey, stranger. It's been a while. How are things on Wall Street?

JOHN: Dangerous. I'm hunting elephants as we speak.

LUCINDA: How is that possible, baby? You know I'm vegan and now we can't elope. (*flirty*)

John looks at Skylar with a dumbfounded expression, then turns back to Lucinda.

JOHN: Princess, it's a term we use on Wall Street referring to landing new business.

LUCINDA: I forgive you. (*laughs*) Lets toast to your return, a round of shots on the house.

Lucinda makes the shots

JOHN: And who are you? (*turns his face to Skylar*)

SKYLAR: You don't remember me?

JOHN: I can't remember every beautiful blonde I come into contact with. I would be divorced and broke.

SKYLAR: I will give you one clue. My name starts with an S.

JOHN: Sophia

SKYLAR: No, guess again.

JOHN: You do look Italian. I just had way too much coke and booze last time I was here. Your face seems familiar.

Lucinda comes back with a round of tequila shots and distracts John's conversation with Skylar.

LUCINDA: "Tequila Nights..."

(All toast)

Skylar isn't much of a drinker, especially when it comes to hard liquor shots, but she reminds herself she is playing the role of the exotic dancer, "Soleil" tonight, so saying no is out of the question. She swallows a quarter of the shot and then tries to distract John, so he won't notice she took only a quarter of the shot. She quickly moves the shot to the other side without him noticing, and then begins to order more liquor. Skylar favors sweeter drinks where you can't taste the alcohol.

SKYLAR: Can I get a tequila sunrise?

LUCINDA: Coming right up.

JOHN: So, it's a tequila night?

SKYLAR: It's a wild night.

JOHN: I would like to hear more about this wild night.

Skylar gets closer to John, looks at him seductively and starts to put her hands around him, touching him in a seductive way.

SKYLAR: It's a wild night that is going to make you hard and happy. (*She moves her hand subtly toward his private area*) Do you remember me now?

JOHN: Yes, I do. You are Lola's puppet.

SKYLAR: I'm no longer a puppet. I graduated to a blonde bombshell named Soleil, and I'm going to be your fantasy tonight. How does that sound? (*touches him more seductively*)

JOHN: Amazing, but I'm shocked. You seem completely different. Even your smell.

Skylar is using scented oils of vanilla, amber, and cinnamon which, she discovered, activates the pheromones of her male customers.

SKYLAR: My scent is a Wall Street magnet. I told you I graduated to blonde bombshell, so what do you say to a bubbly champagne room?

Lucinda comes back, interrupting their conversation.

LUCINDA: Tequila sunrise and John, this one is on Redmond (*she points near the club entrance where Redmond is standing with the headset for security*)

John nods to Redmond from afar, acknowledging his drink. Redmond signals with one finger that he will be coming over in one minute.

JOHN: No champagne tonight. I have to be up early and can't get in trouble. I love your new look. I will definitely play next time.

SKYLAR: If I'm not in a room with the Onyx Equities guys, then I'm yours, baby.

John interrupts Skylar in a drunken, angry tone

JOHN: If that's how you play, then your loss. I got news for you, blondie: they are a piece of shit and if you hang out with them long enough, they will ruin your new look.

Skylar pauses and listens to John's warning and all of sudden, Lucinda came to the rescue.

LUCINDA: Keep it down, Johnny. Brooks Kennedy is here all the time and he is one of our biggest spenders.

JOHN: Big spender, my ass! I have spent over $400,000 on booze, blow and dancers this year, not to mention our annual Christmas holiday party where I racked up another $150,000 on the AmEx.

LUCINDA: Baby, relax. You are number one. I'm going to get another round of tequila on the house. (*goes back to the bar*).

From the doors, Redmond sees John getting heated and he tells the security he will be right back. Redmond is second in charge at Silver Lights and nicknamed "Hawk" because of his quick response to putting out fires before they happen.

Unfortunately, Redmond's talent for catching predators outside the club when it came to more hidden matters like money laundering, failed. This particular incident happened right under Redmond and Tony's eyes for the past two years. Either an unidentified employee, third party or silent investor was giving the Louis Mazarati firm information from their books, including bank accounts, tax statements and private funds that would easily allow Silver Lights to be a participating party in money laundering.

Soon Redmond's days of being a Hawk would be outnumbered by his days playing Sherlock Homes, cleaning up the shit left behind from the crooked employee or investor. But first he had to charm the pants off John Marino and coax him into spending $10K in the Howard Stern champagne room, to make the club's quota for the night.

DIALOGUE

SKYLAR: Whoa, baby, I didn't mean to upset you. I won't ever mention his name again.

JOHN: Now I remember you clearly, it's all coming back. The erotic lap dance you and Lola gave me. Where is she?

SKYLAR: Lola is at a film festival for her new documentary.

Just as Skylar says that, Anastasia pops her head from out of nowhere. She is known as "Elizabeth" at Silver Lights and she is with Phillip Delfonte, an executive and close friend who works with John Marino at Sapphire Investments.

Philip Delfonte, in City of Dreams, was left on cliff when he found out his wife, Cassandra Delfonte (now soon to be ex-wife) was having an extra-marital affair with Brooks Kennedy, an associate of his rival firm, Onyx Equities. The entire time, Cassandra was giving

Brooks information about Sapphire Investments that Brooks was using for financial gain, creating a monopoly over the technology sector. A divorce was in the making and Cassandra shortly realized that Brooks Kennedy used his good looks and his playboy charm to get what he needed. Once he got the information, the self-absorbed prick kicked her to the curb like yesterday's trash. She begged Philip to give her another chance, saying she would do anything to win him back, but it was too late. The damage was done. Two weeks later, she moved out, leaving Philip Delfonte to the pack of wolves in Silver Lights. Soon, he had not just one dancer in his lap, but two!

Now, Philip's spending at Silver Lights is spiralling out of control, his booze habit and sex addiction feeding his reckless spending habits. His daily blowjobs in the champagne room are costing him a $1000 a girl, plus the cost of the room and extra tips for privacy. He is getting a reputation as "the Blow Job King" around the club.

Right behind him in the far upper left VIP section is Craig Peters. Craig Peters is a bit more cautious about his reputation at Silver Lights and his spending. From time to time he can be coerced into a room. Of all the Wall Street guys, he's never married and is somewhat more soft-spoken than his associates. There is a rumor he is starting to become a Sugar Daddy to one of the dancers at the club, and he is definitely giving her some "sugar" for her bills outside the club. No one knows who it is. Craig comes in and flirts with a variety of dancers, from blondes to brunettes, and he prefers to be in a relationship that is more like the typical sugar baby arrangement. The life of marriage and kids does not fit his New York lifestyle. His heart was broken early in his youth by his high school girlfriend, and again by a fiancé whom he caught cheating with his best friend. From then *on, Craig, who resembled Bruce Willis, vowed he would never get emotionally close again or let his guard down.*

Anastasia hears pieces of the conversation and being that she isn't a fan of Lola, has to put her last word in.

ANASTASIA: Lola is with her new sugar daddy, Chris Banks. The big shot who runs all of Graphite Entertainment.

JOHN: Technically, it's not his business, dear. It's his dad's, Chris Senior. Junior rides off the coattails of his rich dad's name to get sugar babies just like Lola.

LUCINDA: That's bullshit! Lola is in attendance at the film festival with her new agent Susan Banks, who is Chris Banks' sisters. *(looking at Anastasia)*

John knows both Chris and Susan Banks through the entertainment world of New York City. Chris Banks is Steven Banks' cousin, who is a key player in the merger of Gemstone Hospitality with Diamond Hospitality, giving Silver Lights the potential to become a national franchise.

John Marino is disappointed after hearing Lola is out with a new sugar daddy, but when he sees Phillip Delfonte behind Anastasia, he forgets.

PHILLIP: Hey, stranger.

JOHN: What are you doing here?

PHILLIP: I just finished working on the potential merger for Vital Pharmaceuticals, the company owned by Grant Lawrence, and just wanted to grab a drink with the boys. (*referring to Sapphire Investment associates in his group*).

John looks over and notices someone different in the crowd.

JOHN: Who is that? He doesn't look like a Sapphire associate.

ANASTASIA: That's Pierre Luca. You don't know who he is?

JOHN: The French socialite and billionaire who has been linked to every *Page Six* model or actress. Why in the hell are you hanging out with that buffoon?

PHILLIP: That buffoon's family owns 85 percent shares of Randall Pharmaceuticals, which is the "it" company to acquire on Wall Street.

JOHN: The French company that's about to launch a new immuno-therapy drug for cancer?

PHILLIP: Yes.

JOHN: Does "the Beast of Wall Street" know about this?

PHILLIP: I haven't said anything to Charles, because I want to see how the meeting goes.

JOHN: I'm glad to see someone is doing their job. I have a few meetings tomorrow where I'll need my A game, so I'm going to be heading out soon.

Redmond comes into the scene.

REDMOND: My favorite crew. Lucinda, get a round of bombshells.

JOHN: Red, I don't need any more bombshells. I had enough bombshells the past eight weeks to last me a lifetime, especially the one from Onyx Equities. Besides, I have a bigger bombshell named Gabriella waiting at home and she will go off if I don't get home right now.

Lucinda prepares the bombshell drinks which consist of tequila, lime juice, raspberry liqueur, a splash of apple juice and a slice of lime.

REDMOND: It's been too long though. We have rooms going on tonight for half off, with a free champagne bottle for the first hour.

John looks at Philip, then turns his head toward Skylar, and then back to Redmond.

JOHN: It sounds tempting but I'm going to have to pass. I have early meetings.

REDMOND: OK, but don't forget about our annual masquerade party next Thursday. It's going to be a night to remember, with a surprise porn star performance on stage and an undisclosed celebrity appearance. Right now, we are sold at 60 percent capacity, so the sooner you let me know about attending, we can reserve you a room.

PHILLIP: You can reserve me a room.

JOHN: Phil, hold off for now. I just want to check with Gabriella to make sure we have no events. Also, I want to see if the Beast wants to attend through the back door. It's actually the perfect opportunity for him to be in a disguise and play.

Redmond can't believe his ears that Charles Marziano, the Beast of Wall Street will possibly be attending the biggest party of the year. This could be the break Silver Lights deserves in terms of national exposure, bringing Steve Banks' investment offer of Gemstone Hospitality to the table. Last but not least, it's the thrill that Skylar's screenplay, Hollywood Dreams needs.

All of sudden, John gets a text from his wife, Gabriella, asking when he was coming home.

JOHN: I need to run. Here's for the drinks (*hands the bartenders a few hundred-dollar bills*). Red, I will let you know soon about the room for next week.

John heads out and Redmond turns his attention to Skylar, Phillip and Anastasia. Skylar's heart begins to race as her face flushes while Redmond speaks.

REDMOND: Are you going to do a champagne room tonight?

PHILLIP: I think we are going to pass and wait for the masquerade party to do one. We are hanging out in the VIP area with Mr. Playboy (*winks and looks back over there*).

RED: You can't go wrong when you have Luca in the house.

ANASTASIA: Soleil come and join us.

SKYLAR: Once I finish my bombshell.

REDMOND: By the way, Soleil, something looks different about you.

SKYLAR: I became a blonde bombshell (*winks*)

REDMOND: It compliments you.

Just as Skylar's heart is about to come out of her chest, Redmond compliments her, and just like that, the name "Soleil" echoes across the speaker by DJ Pauly.

Redmond really can't stop looking at her toned legs, and how nice her ass looks. The blonde hair really takes her new character "Soleil" to a new level of sexiness. He is completely taken aback at how hot she looks. He has to snap himself out of his sexual fantasy. Meanwhile, Skylar is doing an excellent job in her new role as "Soleil," the exotic dancer, by taking her talent as an aspiring actress and screenwriter to another level of praise. Her new character is apparently catching the eyes of important people, including the countryman, Redmond, as well as John Marino, a key character in the brewing Wall Street rivalries.

Skylar takes a few steps forward, moving toward the stage as all eyes are on her new character, "Soleil," and from out of nowhere, she turns around, staring straight at the Wall Street boys.

"Just wait until I get off," she says. "It's going to be a tequila kind of night."

FADE OUT

CHAPTER 5
DANCING QUEEN

Seven weeks passed, and the small-town girl, Skylar Lynn was no longer small-town as she graduated from innocent girl in *City of Dreams* to a sultry exotic dancer in *Hollywood Dreams*, earning her quite the reputation as "the Dance Queen." You could see everything in her new role illustrated a Dance Queen, from the way her long blonde hair cascaded down her back to the way she took to the pole and moved her hips in the sultriest of ways. Her routine mimicked a professional dancer as she started to visualize her dance routines as if she was performing on *Dancing with The Stars*. This visualization technique she used, along with the supernatural powers emanating from the Silver Heels, gave her new role excitement and high energy as she danced toward her *Hollywood Dreams*.

This time around, instead of the *Silver Lights* guiding the Dancing Queen to finish *Hollywood Dreams*, the supernatural power of *the Silver Heels* led Skylar's dance steps every beat of the way. *The Silver Heels*, just like *the Silver Lights*, gave Skylar faith to dance into the spotlight, as her performance was one headline away to breaking her *Page Six* story.

Indeed, she took Javier's advice from *City of Dreams* that her new role was more than just a stripper, but a role of a lifetime for her talent to shine across *Hollywood Dreams*, so one day she would be dancing the night away at *the Golden Globes* in her final feature, *the Golden Dream.*

In order for Skylar Lynn to finish *Hollywood Dreams* with success, she would have to capture the attention of the famous French billionaire and playboy Pierre Luca, earn a Silver Invitation to become his "princess" and submissive in the world the rich and famous and then, break a *Page Six* story that would spotlight her *Hollywood Dreams.*

The lifestyle of the rich and famous was a world foreign to this Midwestern girl who came from humble beginnings. Her life growing up was the farthest thing from private jets, designer clothes, unlimited spending and posh trips. Soon enough, she would find out some of the skeletons to some of the richest and most powerful people, stuff that *Page Six* Stories couldn't write about, but only aspiring Hollywood stars could spotlight in a feature screenplay.

BACK TO THE DRAMA

Skylar was dancing erotically on stage, living up to her new reputation as "the Dancing Queen." All eyes were on her, especially the lustful eyes of the world-famous billionaire and socialite, Pierre Luca.

ACT I, SCENE 4
FRENCH DESIRE

FADE IN

All the attention was on Skylar's petite frame and charismatic energy as she performed to house music, seductively shaking her hips against the pole, gyrating with the music and wrapping one leg around the pole as her movement slowed down rhythmically to the music, creating a sultry dance. She channeled her third eye, awakening the powerful force of the Silver Heels, once again giving her performance the energy it needed to shine.

The sultry moves of Skylar Lynn caught the ocean blue eyes of the handsome French billionaire, Pierre Luca. After the tequila shots, his body got warmer and he started to get aroused by Skylar's erotic moves. His sexual urges propeled him to move closer to center stage, so he could show his appreciation by tipping Skylar hundreds. She took her body to the floor, kneeling down, still moving her hips seductively to the beat as she turned her ass to the side of Pierre Luca. He began to tip her two hundred-dollar bills at each side of her thong.

DIALOGUE

PIERRE LUCA: I haven't seen you around. What's your name?

SKYLAR: Soleil.

PIERRE LUCA: Soleil, I like what I see. I'm man of exquisite taste. I know when I see a rare diamond.

Skylar starts blushing and she can't believe Pierre Luca, the youngest billionaire in the world, was acknowledging her. She begins to blush and the whole scene feels like it's out of the movie Pretty Woman.

SKYLAR: Thank you.

PIERRE LUCA: When you get off stage stop by *(looks to where Anastasia, Craig, Phillip, and a few Wall Street guys are sitting)* I would like to talk more.

He tips her another $200 and Skylar is shocked this young billionaire and famous playboy takes interest in her and just tipped her $400. As the song ends, she starts to get butterflies in her stomach thinking about what she will say to him. Her mind starts to forget her twin flame Redmond and just like that, her thoughts are on her new crush, Pierre Luca.

She goes back to the dressing room to quickly touch up her lipstick, powder her face and brush her hair. She looks in the mirror and reminds herself she needs to step into her sultry character "Soleil," and push the quirky screenwriter Skylar out of her head. She takes one deep breath and focuses on the magical powers of the Silver Heels to guide her as "Soleil," the exotic dancer. She heads out of the dressing room toward the upper VIP section where the music is the loudest, and laughter and banter are at a new high among the Wall Street boys.

Pierre Luca warmly greets her. They are sitting in the crimson red plush chairs with the charcoal black tables in the center. Spread across the tables are bottles of tequila, vodka, and mixers.

DIALOGUE

PIERRE LUCA: Mon amour, you were fabulous up there. I haven't seen moves like that in a while.

SKYLAR: It comes naturally.

PIERRE LUCA: I can see that.

Anastasia notices Pierre Luca's attraction to Skylar and interrupts their conversation.

ANASTASIA: Hey, sexy, are you coming to our masquerade ball next Thursday?

PIERRE LUCA: It depends if I have a date.

SKYLAR: You don't need a date. There will be plenty options here to have fun with. (*She winks at him*)

PIERRE LUCA: Would that date be you? (*looks at Skylar*)

ANASTASIA: It could be two for the price of one! (*she touches Pierre Luca*)

Skylar starts to get annoyed because Anastasia is ruining her organic chemistry with Pierre Luca.

PIERRE LUCA: Soleil, are you a threesome type of girl or one-on-one?

SKYLAR: Baby, I'm one-on-one all the way when it comes to a French hunk! I don't like to share my men, especially when they look like you.

CRAIG DELFONTE: Take her into the room. This one is on me.

Anastasia is fuming with jealousy and Skylar can't believe the words that are actually coming out of her mouth. Skylar has what she's getting herself into. She has no real experience when it came to a one-on-one room, versus a group room.

PIERRE LUCA: What do you say, Soleil? You want to make one for the books?

SKYLAR: I have never been more ready.

PIERRE LUCA: Let's go to Michael Donahue and get things squared away for the hour.

The two headed in the direction of the host stand and the VIP room area.

Skylar can't believe the words that are coming out of her tongue. She is literally becoming more turned on each time Pierre speaks. Her crush on Redmond was no longer in her vision. Weirdly enough all she could think about was getting it on with this hunk who looked exactly like Liam Hemsworth. His piercing blue eyes, chiseled face, thick sandy brown hair, and a muscular body to die for were taking Skylar's new character, Soleil, to a whole new level of desire.

It also didn't hurt that this famous French billionaire had a reputation of being a Porn star in the bedroom and his spending on a girl mirrored the fairytale from the acclaimed movie Pretty Woman, where Richard Gere lavishly spoils Julia Roberts. No wonder that outside the club, he had the reputation as "The Knight in Shining Amour" when it came to rescuing a modern-day Cinderella like Skylar.

FADE OUT

Part of Pierre Luca's allure was his background of mega wealth and power. He came from an ultra-rich family with strong political ties all over Europe and the USA. His family had money other people only dreamed of. Private jets, mansions, butlers, a private staff, unlimited bank accounts, luxury cars, a network of rich people, celebrities and politicians that were only a phone call away. No wonder he felt like he could be himself in a place like Silver Lights, because no one would judge him. On the other hand, he could never play out his fantasies with porn, fetish, and role play in the world of high society, because if his sex addiction ever came out, it would be shunned. His deepest desires were with ladies like Skylar, who came from the other end of the woods, opposite of his upbringing. She could be his submissive and he could play the Dom. He just loved girls he could be himself with, girls who would be happy to be his submissive, following his commands.

His darkest fantasies were only halfway met at Silver Lights, whereas the other half of his desires would be met with Skylar in his fantasy suite at his penthouse apartment. There she would learn to how to play a submissive, explore her partner's darkest desires, while also having a deeper understanding of the world of erotic fantasy, so the second half of *Hollywood Dreams* would have an erotic twist that would set her apart from the millions of aspiring Hollywood writers and actresses she would be going up against in getting her feature on the big screen.

Pierre Luca had heard about Skylar's first feature, *City of Dreams*. He did his research and found out that she studied acting and had been writing for years. She had been pitching *City of Dreams* to a few producers and entertainment agents. One of them was Susan Banks. Pierre Luca was so powerful that if Skylar played her cards right as his submissive in the upcoming acts, she would have the doors open in getting her first movie deal. It would be the flashback of Skylar's scenes in her soap opera nights that would shift the tone of her second feature in making it a jaw-dropping blockbuster.

CHAPTER 6

SOAP OPERA NIGHTS

In the underground world of exotic entertainment, each night at Silver Lights mirrored a steamy soap opera, including sexual escapades in the champagne rooms, to heated love affairs between Silver Lights employees, to Wall Street initiation parties containing threesomes. There was so much material and dialogue that Skylar had to be careful to select those scenes which would make *Hollywood Dreams* a hit!

You name it, Skylar saw it. From threesomes to blow being snorted off stripper's boobs to fetish parties in the Howard Stern champagne room. Nothing was off-limits, and the more money someone spent in the room, the more the staff turned a blind eye. Each night the supernatural powers of *the Silver Heels* guided her through the steamiest of nights. She couldn't believe her eyes when she saw office sex between Michael Donahue and "the Queen Bee," Lola, and of course, Redmond's forbidden affairs with the weekly porn features.

The love affair brewing between Michael and Lola had been happening for a while. Michael's bad boy ways turned Lola on so much that one night while she was working, she came on to him strongly. She cornered him in the back office and stripped down to nothing. The two had sex in just about every position and the rest was history. The orgasms Michael gave her blurred her vision for a real relationship outside the club. The sex was so good and his bad boy image heightened her climax every time. He knew her body so well, he could make her have multiple orgasms in a short time, living up to his reputation as a rock star in the bedroom. She literally became more obsessed with him, the more she fucked him in the club, and there was a big upside to being Michael's girlfriend: the high rollers that he pushed her way. Michael gave Lola first bids on all the top spenders under the condition she would give him a 20% cut of her profits. This was customary when a champagne host hooked up a dancer with a big spender.

It also didn't hurt that Michael was devilishly handsome to sleep with, a face that resembled Leo DiCaprio. His piercing blue eyes from his Irish side and olive skin from his Italian heritage made him quite the looker, along with a body that matched an athlete's. He had no fat and he worked out religiously at the gym to make sure his jacked body matched his bad boy image. He was quite the sales guy with words. Charming and convincing to say the least, no matter whom he talked to.

Over time, Michael grew attached to Lola, but she knew he would never leave his wife, Grace, and daughter, Hayley. His wife was a former cover model and actress who turned a blind eye to Michael's ways for a life of luxury. If only she knew that his new role as the silent shaker and maker to back end Wall Street deals could lead to deadly consequences, she might not be so blind.

FLASHBACK: 7 WEEKS AGO, FROM THE CITY OF DREAMS

THE FOOT FETISH ROOM WITH STEVEN BANKS

You couldn't overlook the steamy scenes between the power fueled Wall Street guys and select dancers. The more money that bank-rolled the Wall Street guys, the hungrier their appetite became for blow, sex, and fetish! Many high-powered executives came in for dominatrix sessions, foot fetish parties and role play fantasy. Nothing was off limits, as Skylar observed first-hand in her first fetish room at Silver Lights. It was a foot fetish party with Steven Banks, a stocky middle-aged American business guy that looked like the actor Danny DeVito. He had a greasy, receding hair line, blue eyes and reddish skin from drinking too much bourbon. He was known to have diarrhea of the mouth with his outlandish comments and eccentric sense of humor, often getting him in trouble while making him the talk of the night!

Skylar's first champagne room was with Steven Banks and there were two other girls in the room also, Bri, and Lola. Bri was the most exotic-looking dancer at Silver Lights, her face a combination of pop singer Rihanna and celebrity Alicia Keys. An aspiring artist in the field of music, she looked at every champagne room as an opportunity to further her career. She was fairly easy to get along with, until someone messed with her money.

Lola, known as "the Queen Bee" of Silver Lights was an expert when it came to dealing with high net worth clients like Steven Banks or Brooks Kennedy. This Queen Bee was going to direct the girls with Steven. She took out her stash of blow, given by Michael Donahue, and spread it across her tits for Steven to snort. Then the bottle waitress came in with a round of tequila shots. Between the three lines of blow, and the shots, Steven began to slur his words about licking and sucking Lola's feet. Right then and there, Lola placed her feet near his mouth as all the girls began rotating their feet like musical chairs, so he could have a heyday with their feet. He even had Lola perform a hand job with her feet. Skylar was shocked to see how one high powered executive could be so turned on by feet, not a vagina, ass or even tits.

Skylar took Lola's lead in the room by putting whipped cream on her tits and feet, then spraying the champagne on Steven's cock for lubrication. Bri and Lola proceeded to make out with each other in front him. After that, Lola attempted to do a foot hand job, using her perfectly pedicured feet to stroke his cock. The more she stroked her feet on his cock, the louder his moans became. That night ended with a nice happy ending from Steven and a fat tip of $3,000 apiece. His stocky body waddled loudly out as he was on cloud nine. His loud banter and big tips to management eased both Tony and Redmond's worry about Diamond Hospitality's investment. Now all that was left to spotlight back in *The City of Dreams* during this flashback was the finicky socialite, Brooks Kennedy.

FLASHBACK: 7 WEEKS AGO, FROM *THE CITY OF DREAMS*
THE HOWARD STERN CHAMPAGNE ROOM WITH BROOK'S
KENNEDY

Brooks Kennedy wanted nothing to do with feet and was all about wild sex. He had a large appetite for variety and role play. His high-powered role of running one of the largest hedge funds on Wall Street left little time for play in the world of adult entertainment. He secretly loved escorts and had a thing for strip clubs because he felt free to explore his darkest desires. His clean-cut, all-American looks resembled famous hunk Jamie Dornan. His thick, light brown hair and ocean blue eyes could make any girl go into a daydream. It was obvious he had no trouble attracting the cream of the crop when it came to the hottest women in New York City. Unlike Steven Banks' champagne room of wet feet, Brooks' rooms at Silver Lights were more like real porn. He usually popped in whenever he had a craving for sex (reservations were only made ahead time for important clients like Grant Lawrence, CEO of Vital Pharmaceuticals). This was the case the day of Steven Banks' wild foot party!

In *City of Dreams*, there was a dilemma of the overlap between Steven Banks and Brooks Kennedy's room reservations, but that didn't even occur because of Lola's extra sweet party favors of blow and her wild foot hand job making it a glorious night for the books with a $50,000 dollar tip to management from Steven Banks and $30,000 from Brooks Kennedy.

Brooks, on the other hand, wanted nothing in the realms of a foot fantasy party, he preferred the real thing. He usually got a blow job or a quickie with a bag of cocaine. Only dancers willing to get down and be extra dirty for his voracious appetite of sex would make the cut. He also had a thing for porn stars. He loved watching porn regularly with whomever he was dating and one of his favorites was Amber Ray. The night he came into Silver Lights with Grant Lawrence, he messaged Michael Donahue ahead of time, saying he wanted his usual: a bag of coke, a bottle of the best tequila and two dancers that were willing do extras. He mentioned a nice bonus if Redmond could get one of their feature porn stars to join.

When it came to getting dirty, Brooks loved all flavors of woman including spicy Latina, kinky Asian and of course, the submissive

Catholic girls. Brooks was a hardcore sex addict and anything that got his cock hard he was ready to fuck. It just depended on what his sexual appetite was craving that particular night and how much blow he did. Secretly, he fantasized of being a porn star, having sex with tons of chicks in different roles, but it would never fly in his world. Born into old money, with a political name to uphold, his reputation of high New York society was the backbone to his hustle, so no wonder his sex addiction got fed to its fullest behind the doors at Silver Lights.

The night Brooks came in, Anastasia, known as "Elizabeth" at Silver Lights, was brought into the room. It was a night to remember as Brooks got a real treat, a real-life porn star. Brooks had price limit for the right porn fantasy, and that porn star just happened to be the one and only Amber Ray.

Amber was quite the stunner, not just in looks but in wit too. She had long dark hair, olive skin, strong features and a body to kill for. She had long, lean legs and a huge rack of implants that just took any man's breath away. She was a former Ivy Leaguer and came from a public relations background in New York City. She started exploring the underground world of sex with high powered politicians and celebrities as a high-end escort. She entered the world of porn by accident with a real-life date. One night she was out with one of the most famous male models on the circuit, Levi Sanchez. During their hot and heavy make out session, the two were watching porn and both expressed mutual desires to make their own porn. In the heat of passion, she blurted out "Let's make a porn."

Being that Levi Sanchez was a free spirit and a sex symbol already in the modeling industry, he thought a sex video, if done right, could be a life changer, and it was. The two got extremely lucky in that it was bought out and brokered to the porn king of adult entertainment, *Vivid Entertainment,* who made both of them an offer they couldn't resist, including a lucrative salary, future royalties, and the chance to star exclusively in other vivid movies, creating a following overnight. To make a long story short, Amber's public relations career washed away with the thunderstorm of her career as a top porn star, and Levi's modeling career was taken by storm too, tripling his bank account.

Anastasia looked nothing like a porn star. She was a voluptuous blonde who had quite the booty and a set of sex lips to match that ass of hers. Rumors were running rampant around the club about her reputation as "the Happy Ending Dancer." Every week in the club, like many of the dancers, Anastasia had lofty goals that needed to be met. Therefore, unlike some of her peers, she was willing to go the extra mile to make sure she was meeting her goals. She was under pressure at home from footing her own bills to investing in her boyfriend, Trey's technology business. His business was a technology platform focusing on minimizing food waste and increasing the bottom line for restaurants in such a way that created outsourcing opportunities. Although she was hustling both in the club and at real estate, she saw a huge potential in this platform that one day would be her saving grace to leave dancing once and for all. In the back her mind, her biggest investors were Tony Murano, Partner at Diamond Hospitality and Silver Lights, and his VIP customer, Steven Banks, President of Gemstone Hospitality.

WHERE THE STEAM STARTED

The world of Silver Lights steamed up the night Brooks Kennedy brought his customer, Grant Lawrence, CEO of Vital Pharmaceuticals to his playground in *City of Dreams*. These scenes captured the behind-the-scenes world of adult entertainment like never before, giving Skylar her first taste of a real porn, and her first dialogue of *dirty talk*, one between an egotistical Wall Street playboy and all his flavors of the week.

ACT II SCENE 1
DIRTY TALK

FADE IN

FLASHBACK: 7 WEEKS AGO

INT: HOWARD STERN CHAMPAGNE ROOM

Skylar stumbles nervously into the Howard Stern champagne room. In one area there is a glass armoire full of sex toys, erotic oils, role play costumes, and porn videos. Red velour couches are on each side of a dark grey table. A large, crystal chandelier hangs from the ceiling, perfectly dimmed so one can still see what is going on, but to a passer-by, it appears dark. There is a large TV screen with a DVD player showing topless dancers on stage from inside the club. The music is loud, so you can still hear the dialogue but also appreciate the musical beats. On the table, there are two bottles of Dom Perignon and the best tequila money can buy.

For a moment, no one notices Skylar's presence in the room. Brooks Kennedy is snorting blow off Amber Ray's flat stomach and in the other corner, Anastasia is giving a blow job to Grant Lawrence. Brooks picks his head up after snorting a line of coke, high as a kite, and notices Skylar standing near the TV screen.

DIALOGUE

BROOKS KENNEDY: Hey, baby... What's your name?

SKYLAR: Soleil.

BROOKS KENNEDY: I love French woman. They are a smoke show in the bedroom. Are you ready to play with the best?

(he is touching Amber's underwear and massaging her as he says it)

SKYLAR: What makes you the best?

BROOKS KENNEDY: Well for one thing, I have a big cock! I can also make you cum more times than average dick. I can take you to fucking Disneyland and back for the ride of your life *(looking at his crotch, and then Skylar)* and give you a fantasy that only Cinderellas like yourself dream of. But I won't date you.

SKYLAR: Sounds tempting. Who said anything about dating?

BROOKS KENNEDY: Are you already turning me down before the night begins? I don't take rejection well.

SKYLAR: I'm not turning you down. I have an important meeting I can't be late for in the morning.

BROOKS KENNEDY: $5,000 for the rest of the night.

Skylar hears $5,000 and her mind tells her soul, "Yes." She needs this money for her piling bills and to get out of debt. She knows if she *can twist the dialogue around with her words, she can be the viewer rather than the performer.*

AMBER RAY: Please reconsider, babe. We have a ton of blow and you are just my type when it comes to having fun with girls.

Skylar swallows nervously, thinking of the hot mess she is getting herself into.

SKYLAR: I would love to play, but I was actually on my way to see Redmond and by accident, stumbled in here.

Anastasia hears the familiar voice of Skylar.

ANASTASIA: Soleil, what in god's name are you doing here?

BROOKS KENNEDY: She is going to join us tonight in our group orgy and coke party.

GRANT LAWRANCE: While you're giving out invites, we should text Redmond to get us a redhead. I have a thing for gingers. They give the best blow jobs.

ANASTASIA: Excuse me, your eyes just about rolled back before we got interrupted. I give one hell of a happy ending!

GRANT LAWRANCE: I'm sure you do. I have a big fetish for redheads!

ANASTASIA: Soleil is new here and doesn't understand how the champagne rooms operate.

Skylar's personality immediately shifts to one oozing with confidence and sex appeal. She remembers the warning from the other dancers in City of Dreams, about Anastasia creating conflict and messing with their money.

SKYLAR: Elizabeth, I may be new but I'm no amateur when it comes to getting naughty.

Anastasia looks at Skylar with shock and envy, no longer recognizing the soft-spoken Midwestern girl.

BROOKS KENNEDY: I like the way you are talking. I'm going to let Redmond know we have you for the hour and I will give you $5,000.

Out of nowhere, there is a knock on the door from assistant host, Frankie Martinez, known as "Smooth Frankie" around the club because he is smooth in selling champagne rooms and schmoozing with top customers every night, selling around $15,000 dollars a week in liquor sales. He is in his late twenties, part Italian and Spanish, with looks that resemble Mark Consuelo. During the day, he works on his music album and dreams of being known as a top recording artist. He has family ties to the mob and Frank Delucca is his relative. No one know exactly what the relation is, whether uncle or distant cousin, only that Frank Delucca sends Smooth Frankie high-spending mob customers.

AMBER RAY: Hey, stranger, so nice to see you. Come join our sinful fantasy.

FRANKIE MARTINEZ: I love sinful fantasies. So much that I need to know if you are in for another hour?

BROOKS KENNEDY: Yes, and I want Soleil here for the hour. You can give her $5,000 in dance dollars.

Dance dollars are a credit for the dancer, redeemed at the end of the night in cash or check.

FRANKIE MARTINEZ: Are you ready to have fun for the hour?

SKYLAR: Yes.

GRANT LAWRANCE: Can you also see if there are any sexy gingers out on the floor? I have a real fetish for redheads.

FRANKIE MARTINEZ: I have the perfect dancer. Her name is Kaitlynn. She is submissive and has an A-plus reputation in dirty talk.

AMBER RAY: I have an A-plus reputation for best screen performance. What is your A-plus reputation in? (*She goes up to Frankie and touches the buttons of his dress shirt*)

FRANKIE MARTINEZ: I have an A-plus reputation as "the Tongue Master."

AMBER RAY: Oh, baby, you are making me real wet. Why don't you ditch the suit and get in your birthday suit?

FRANKIE MARTINEZ: Not tonight, but once Kaitlynn comes in, things will get hot.

Kaitlynn is a full-time nursing student, and part-time internet model. She is in her mid-twenties, with fair skin, long strawberry blonde hair, and Norwegian features. She has been dancing for a few years and pretty much knows how to take a champagne room from vanilla to rocky road within minutes. Her former background as a phone sex operator and web cam stripper makes her the ideal entertainer for a steamy night.

FRANKIE MARTINEZ: Hey, I'm going to get a line before I get back to the floor.

AMBER RAY: Baby, I want you to snort it off my tits.

Frankie snorts blow off Amber's tits. Brooks follows his lead, pouring more blow over her tits and the two men alternate their lines. Skylar notices Grant Lawrence is not doing any drugs. Once they finished their cocaine binge, Frankie leaves to seek out Kaitlynn, charge Brooks' account $5,000 and notify Redmond that Skylar will be doing the room with them.

When Redmond hears that the sweet Midwesterner Skylar is doing her first room with the sexually charged egotistical Brooks Kennedy, he becomes concerned. He knows Brooks' style of foreplay and aggressive sex through the room cameras. Brooks typically starts with a bottle of tequila, followed by lines of cocaine. Then he has full nude lap dances, followed by caressing the girls and getting the girls into each other. Afterwards, he usually finishes his night with sex, depending on who the dancer is or if there is a porn star like Amber. The only time he's satisfied with just a blow job is if he is too fucked up on cocaine and alcohol to keep his dick hard.

Redmond cares deeply enough about Skylar to go out of his way to protect her from being fed to the wolves. He deliberately plans to interrupt the room in fifteen minutes with a house round of tequila shots and a new porn video to distract Brooks' attention away from Skylar.

Skylar's first real taste of a champagne room is happening right before her eyes. On screen, there is a porn video playing and in the background, there is house music playing. Skylar starts dancing for Brooks Kennedy with Amber, letting the power of her Silver Heels protect her spirit from going too far. She can't believe what is happening, that in a matter of seconds she is about to get hot and heavy with a porn star and a handsome socialite.

As she starts dancing for Brooks Kennedy, he grabs her face against his and starts kissing her slow and sensual. He gently slips his tongue into her mouth, locking tongues. He is quite the advanced kisser, and the two start getting in unison with their kisses. Skylar gets turned on but after five minutes, Brooks moves to Amber. Skylar moves to the side as the two really take it up a notch. Brooks takes off Amber's lace underwear and starts massaging her labia and gently stroking her clit, focusing on the right pressure to hit her G spot. She begins to moan and pulls out her strawberry-flavored lube, rubbing it across her clit. Brooks moves his face closer to hers, and the two are sucking face once again, passionately kissing.

Skylar is dancing while this is going on, hoping no one notices her. Suddenly, Brooks stops and looks at her. Skylar starts talking dirty to keep the attention on them. "You guys, I'm getting so turned on watching you. Keep this up, I'm just going to touch my pussy while I watch. Brooks, baby, give me a show. One that will make her scream for your nice hard cock."

Skylar can't believe the words spitting out of her mouth, but it was saving her from doing anything she would regret. She tells herself words are just as powerful as her erotic dance moves in shielding off Brooks' advances. Just like that, the tempo of the music changes and the hot tryst between Brooks and Amber starts back up.

The door opens and lo and behold, a sultry redhead with big boobs named Kaitlynn comes in, escorted by Smooth Frankie. All eyes are on them as she tongues Frankie goodbye. Kaitlynn goes to the table to do a few lines, then she interrupts the sex between Anastasia and Grant.

DIALOGUE

KAITLYNN: I heard you have a thing for gingers.

GRANT LAWRENCE: A thing is an understatement. I have a fantasy.

KAITLYNN: I'm at your command. Let me know how I can serve you in getting more aroused.

ANASTASIA: Baby, can't you see how turned on he is by me?

BROOKS KENNEDY: Kaitlynn, let him finish up. I want you to myself first. Come over here and play with us and when they finish, you can go back to him.

Grant Lawrence looks pissed as he wants to have the redhead Kaitlynn and the voluptuous blonde Anastasia at the same time. However, Brooks always prevails. Kaitlynn moves toward the couch area where Brooks and Amber are making out. She notices Skylar watching from the sidelines and pulls her toward the group.

Katelynn starts kissing Amber while Brooks slides his tongue down Skylar's throat, moving his hand down her chest toward her underwear. It is obvious Skylar is uncomfortable as she moves Brooks hands away from her crotch toward her ass. Kaitlynn stops kissing Amber and tells Skylar, "Get some blow, the climax will be better."

Katelynn moves toward Brooks, pushing Skylar aside, and takes charge by unbuttoning his dress shirt. She runs her hands through his hair wildly and touches his face as she gets completely naked and straddles him. While Amber is snorting coke and drinking champagne, Brooks strips down to boxers. All of sudden, there is a knock on the door and it is the one and only countryman, Redmond. He looks like a twin to Sons of Anarchy star, Charlie Hunnam. A bartender, Lucinda, is at his side, with a round of Bombshell shots.

REDMOND: Bombshells on the house.

BROOKS KENNEDY: Red, you're my best man if I ever get married.

GRANT LAWRENCE: Now you're talking nonsense, that would be end to our business deals. (*sarcastically*)

Lucinda begins to hand out the tequila raspberry liquor shots called Bombshells.

AMBER RAY: Let's toast to Silver Lights.

REDMOND: No let's toast to tequila nights.

Everyone gets their shot and toasts. The only one who doesn't take the shot in full is the Hollywood dreamer and aspiring actress, Skylar Lynn. No one notices except Redmond, her twin flame. He came to rescue Skylar because she isn't ready for what comes next. He figures the round of shots and lines of blow will make Brooks forget about Skylar's non-participation.

GRANT LAWRENCE: That shot was killer!

LUCINDA: It's our new shot called Bombshells. We can make it in a drink too.

REDMOND: I'm not done yet. I came here with a new surprise.

BROOKS KENNEDY: I love surprises.

REDMOND: I have a copy of the new porn, "Stock Girl Shakes up Wall Street" that just got released from *Vivid.*

Redmond puts the new porn on the DVD, and everyone watches with intrigue as Lucinda pours tequila mixers and glasses of champagne. Kaitlynn begins to passionately kiss Grant once the porn comes on, then makes her rotations to Amber and then Brooks. Soon they begin a threesome and Anastasia goes back to Grant in the corner, giving him a blow job so she can live up to her name "the Happy Ending Dancer." Redmond discreetly signals Skylar to leave the room and they quietly sneak out.

Skylar feels the supernatural powers of the Silver Heels protecting her character in the most sinful of scenes. She strongly believes her twin flame, Redmond, felt her soul silently calling for help. He still doesn't understand the level of their soul connection, but what he knows is he felt the need to protect her. It wouldn't be until her final act in Hollywood Dreams that their past life from the 1920s would make sense.

The taste Skylar gets from her first room in City of Dreams left her thirsty for a more erotic storyline in Hollywood Dreams. The erotic storyline awaiting her will unexpectedly take place in the West Village penthouse apartment of French billionaire and playboy, Pierre Luca. Skylar soon will be walking into a sinful fairytale she's long desired with a leading character, arm in arm as the two tango into night.

If she plays her cards right during her fantasy date, Skylar will be granted a Silver Invitation into Pierre's private world of sex, fantasy and desire. Skylar has no clue the sexual adventure awaiting her once she became his "Princess," and he steps into the role of "Dark Knight." He will blow her mind in ways a porn video or tantric techniques can't. His conquest with Skylar is just beginning: first thing on his list is to make Skylar feel like a modern-day Cinderella with expensive lingerie gifts, romantic gestures and orgasmic food that will heat up the fairytale date. Skylar will soon get her first taste of a romantic heroine who knows the art of seduction, kissing, role play and foodgasms.

FADE OUT

CHAPTER 7
SINFUL FAIRYTALES

The world of Silver Lights happened to be a place where all sinful fairytales started. From the moment someone walked into the club, they couldn't help but notice a playground fit for the biggest players. If the red-light ambiance didn't mesmerize, then the nakedly clad dancers on various stages would captivate the imagination. If that wasn't enough, all the fantasy champagne rooms had erotic themes including the Dungeon Room, the Jungle Room, and the signature Howard Stern champagne room, which was for elite customers. For many of the customers at Silver Lights, the sinful fairytales stayed in the champagne-soaked VIP rooms but for many others, it continued outside the club. This happened to be the case for the "Dark Knight," Pierre Luca, the world's youngest billionaire and playboy.

His reputation in the club was "the Knight in Shining Armor," but outside the club and in his penthouse, he was the "Dark Knight." He was selective in who he had eyes for and the lucky chosen gal for his fantasy dates would receive a pair of designer silver heels. Pierre noticed Skylar was special from the start, from the way she moved with the music, connecting the rhythm of her soul to the vibrations of the music. The contagious energy she gave off during each dance performance drew him in like a magnet. He noticed her aura was unique and he could see glimpses of her talent during her stage performance. His curiosity piqued so much that he invited the small-town girl to be his second fantasy date in his penthouse apartment.

THE SINFUL FAIRYTALE STARTS

Once upon a time in the world of sinful fairytales, there comes a Dark Knight that rescues a fantasy or two, and perhaps a dream. For Skylar Lynn, aspiring Hollywood star, her dreams awaited her in the 4,000 square foot West Village penthouse. Skylar had no clue what lay ahead but soon she would learn sinful fairytales came with not just an orgasm but a foodgasm too!

Skylar was more ready then ever when she entered Pierre's foyer. His penthouse was immaculately decorated from floor to ceiling in a contemporary, transitional theme. She was greeted by a huge free-standing naked sculpture in the entrance with several abstract art paintings hanging perfectly across the white walls. It was obvious the theme of sensuality was all over Pierre's home, from the beautiful naked statues to the sensual abstract art that drew one in, yet it was the aromatic scent of food cooking that made Skylar forget where she was.

Pierre was quite the chef, self-taught and conditioned in Europe from a young age to be a culinary wizard. His family owned the largest restaurant company in Europe, so frequently eating at five-star restaurants was the norm. His specialty in culinary food happened to be starters and succulent desserts. To friends and family, he was known as "the Food God." He had a way with creating dishes that literally melted in the mouth and caused one to have a foodgasm! He was known to make this happen on his fantasy dates with his signature dishes.

When it came to areas of romance, Pierre went to all stops, including a bouquet of flowers, expensive lingerie and of course, romantic notes. The dining table had some of his signature items: a perfectly long-stemmed bouquet of red roses, a sensual note placed on a gift and a plate of chocolate-covered strawberries.

Skylar still couldn't believe she was in the presence of one of the youngest and richest bachelors in the world and the best part was he made her feel at home. He had a separate bouquet of white roses behind the kitchen island that he was going to surprise her with. On the dining table there was a bottle of the best champagne, already popped open with two champagne glasses filled, and next to it was a plate of strawberries with whipped cream. There was also a nice size platter of crackers, fine cheeses, olives and of course, his signature chocolate-covered strawberries. Skylar thought she was in a scene right out of a romantic movie. Still in shock that her real-life fantasy was coming true, the thought of her twin flame, Redmond, began to vanish.

Just when things couldn't get better, Pierre called her "Princess." Skylar was the farthest thing from a princess, living in a run-down 1960s studio on the Upper East Side, living paycheck to paycheck, working three jobs to support her existence. She walked to where he was cooking up a few of his signature dishes. He took notice of her outfit: a tightly fitted black dress with nude heels.

Pierre looked even better in his home than at the club. His muscles were popping out of his light blue dress shirt as he was cooking up some exotic food for their fantasy date. His tanned skin was glowing against his pearly white teeth and his ocean blue eyes were sparkling sex appeal. He was dressed in a European suit, which showed off his steel body. His broad shoulders and large hands made Skylar feel protected, sending her in a quick flashback to their first champagne room a few days ago.

FLASHBACK TO THEIR CHAMPAGNE ROOM TWO DAYS AGO

Her champagne room with him was a bit of a tease and the dialogue was in between PG-13 and R. She danced for him seductively with her G-string on and didn't get fully nude. He was trying to get her underwear off but failed. Every time he moved his hands slowly toward her lower bikini area, Skylar nudged his hands toward her ass. She was in no way ready for him to play with her puss, and she wanted to set herself apart from other girls.

He began to get things heated by teasing the right areas. He slowly kissed her neck, peck by peck, then kissed her ear with his nice lips as his tongue slowly started swirling around, hitting the right spots, instantly giving her goose bumps. He began to kiss slowly down her neck as she was beginning to get extremely turned on, pressing his cock against her G-string. She went in for the first kiss. Surprisingly, Skylar was an excellent kisser and extremely skilled in foreplay and kissing, as she studied and practiced tantric intimacy with her lovers. Tantric was the art of sensuality and intimacy by using the breath, mind, and spirit to connect with a lover in an intimate way. Skylar focused on making sure she was synchronizing her breathing, touching, eye contact and kissing with Pierre.

She had her kissing style down to a tee, depending on who she was with and how much organic chemistry was between them. She was vocal about her practice of tantric and if a lover was out of sync, she would communicate to make sure they were in sync.

Being that Pierre was a heartthrob and the ultimate bachelor in the Big Apple, it wasn't hard to predict Skylar's performance would score big points with the French socialite. Pierre instantly noticed her kissing style and foreplay techniques were extraordinary. Unlike other dancers that he went in the champagne rooms with, Skylar was programmed differently. She was always present when fooling around with her men. She always tapped into their aura first, then their mind, body, and spirit. Pierre could feel that from their first few kisses. They were incredible, slow, sensual and in sync, causing Pierre to take the lead, assertively pushing her down on the couch. He got on top of her and started moving his tongue deeply into her mouth, his hand moving more aggressively toward her G-string. Skylar pulled back again and he could feel her reservation in taking things to the next level. "Slow down," she told him.

Pierre was shocked because he was used to getting his way in the champagne rooms. At the same time, he was intrigue, because she was the first dancer to reject his advances, in spite of playing hard to get. Her extraordinary kissing and foreplay techniques took Pierre's breath away and he was willing to wait and take a chance by inviting her to a fantasy date night at his penthouse. He figured he'd let her call the shots at Silver Lights, but once she walked into his fantasy date, he would be calling the shots. He understood she wanted to take things slow since she was new and inexperienced in the champagne rooms. He tried to calm her prudent behavior with reassurances that anything that happened between them in the champagne room was sealed, and he was someone she could trust as he had a lot more to lose.

A young billionaire and heir to the wealthiest business family in Europe, his reputation was constantly watched and scrutinized by the media. He couldn't afford any *Page Six* slip-ups on his secret life of strip clubs, sexual fantasies, escorts and role play. If any of it leaked out to the press, his life could be ruined, and it could be detrimental to his family empire.

For some reason, he was drawn to Skylar's authenticity and her passionate kissing. They both couldn't get enough of their hot and heavy kissing session as their lips and tongues were literally locked for the full hour. As the two were making out, Redmond noticed on the camera that Pierre was behaving himself and taking things slower than usual. Deep down inside, Redmond was jealous, and constantly caught himself watching their room on the surveillance screen. He still didn't understand his deep-rooted feelings for Skylar but the more he watched the screen, the more he wished he was in Pierre Luca's place, tonguing Skylar, caressing her body and getting her wet in such a way she would recognize his touch from their past life in the roaring 20s. Little did Redmond know that it would be right toward Skylar's final scenes in *Hollywood Dreams* that an intense flashback of his and Skylar's previous life would explain their twin flame connection.

When their time in the champagne room came to an end, it left both Pierre and Skylar wanting more. For Pierre, Skylar was a fresh breath of air with her quick wit, authenticity, and warm demure that sparkled even more from *the Silver Heels*. The power of *the Silver Heels* captured Skylar in a whole new light, magnetically drawing him toward her. He saw Skylar blessed with extraordinary talents and it really hit him later that night when he got home. He remembered during the night in the champagne room, as the two were heavily making out, there was a light shining from Skylar's *Silver Heels*, creating a magnetic force that was drawing Pierre toward Skylar. The light tapped into Skylar's sensuality and spiritual realm so intensely, Pierre felt her vibrations with every touch. He picked up her energy so much during their time together that night, he had a vivid dream of her dressed in a gown, accepting a *Golden Globe* award. He couldn't exactly see what category she won, but she held tightly to the Globe as if it symbolized the rebirth of her soul. He could hear the words God, message, purpose and inspiration in her acceptance speech.

Pierre Luca wasn't much of a religious person, but the fact that he had his first vivid dream in about decade only a few hours after leaving Skylar presence, got him believing in a higher power once again, questioning if he too, like the countryman, had a soul connection to this small town woman. He knew in the dream that he was in the audience, sitting at the table for the movie she either wrote, acted in or both. He felt the presence of something greater when he was with Skylar. The dream of her giving a speech and the words he heard in the dream were so moving, it left him in a cold sweat, wanting to learn everything about this Hollywood dreamer. He was going to wait until their second meeting to ask her about this vision.

For Skylar, Pierre represented the galaxy to her dreams. He was experiencing strong visions and feelings about Skylar, likewise Skylar was experiencing feelings of desire for this playboy. He was so powerful in so many realms, from his political upbringing to his family fortune. He was hooked on her kisses and her tantric form of intimacy. She was drawn to his sex appeal and billionaire image. He never met anyone like her and the opposite vibrations she sent got him thinking of the possibilities they could have within his private world of sex, domination and role play.

BEFORE THE FIRST DATE WITH PIERRE LUCA

Skylar went all the way in making herself look like a modern-day Cinderella, so Pierre's mouth would drop the moment she walked into his penthouse. She went to Arturo's salon for the works, including hair, makeup and nails. She told Arturo in confidence about the date and he assured her he would keep his mouth shut. However, during this time, the anonymous Rose Highwater was sitting right in the corner of the salon and Skylar had no clue who she was as she talked openly about her big date with Pierre. Skylar thought Rose Highwater was just another carbon copy of a rich woman that ran with the elite circle of New York City, but little did she know this woman was pretty powerful on the publishing circuit, with strong connections to just about every major news channel in New York and around the world.

After Skylar left, Rose Highwater couldn't help herself and being the gossiper she was, persuaded Arturo to dish details on Skylar by giving him a $1,000 tip on top of her service. Arturo ended up spilling the beans on Skylar, Silver Lights, and Pierre Luca. Rose knew Pierre quite well as they ran in the same circles, and her new boyfriend Brooks Kennedy hung out with Pierre from time to time and they did business together. Rose heard about Silver Lights' reputation through the grapevine as a place where celebrities, Wall Street executives and politicians partied in the champagne rooms in sex fueled orgies and cocaine parties. She was unaware Pierre went there regularly, which gave her the idea that Brooks Kennedy was also a regular customer.

Arturo didn't realize when he opened his big mouth, he was about to set off a loose cannon. Rose Highwater was no amateur in firing up drama, in fact she was an expert! Arturo was going to give her the biggest ammunition: all the details on the Silver Lights annual masquerade ball. He told her how she could access the invitation list which only Tony Murano, Redmond, and Michael Donahue could do. This small secret would plant the seeds to a *Page Six* story that would shake up the world of the rich and famous. Rose was well-versed in playing the role of detective and gathering information in a sly way. Not only did Arturo mention it was the biggest party of the year, but he also mentioned who would be attending. Michael Kennedy, Brooks Kennedy, Grant Lawrence, Steven Banks, Pierre Luca and Charles Marziano, "the Beast of Wall Street." This conversation was enough dirt for Rose Highwater to start thinking of her next breakthrough Page Six story, one that could make Brooks Kennedy possibly pop the question, or worse, rattle up Skylar's second feature *Hollywood Dreams*.

Rose Highwater was a natural born beauty with silky blonde hair and looks similar to a young Sharon Stone. She had a statuesque, lean body to match her all-American beauty. She craved drama and attention at any cost due to her own insecurities. She couldn't keep a fiancé longer than a month, because of her high drama and high maintenance personality. Her looks definitely got her attention, but it was her drama that got her a reputation. A former contributing editor at the New York Post, she had all the connections to just snap her fingers and make a simple call to break a story and ruin someone's life. She also had a thing for trying to tame rich wild boys like Brooks to settle down. Her record for broken engagements had hit an ultimate high of ten, so relationships were not her strong suit and if things didn't work out, she had a way of making her ex-partner's life a living hell. If Brooks Kennedy didn't become her fiancé, Pierre Luca was the next victim on her list. Meanwhile, Arturo would soon learn karma was a bitch, and the price for opening his big mouth to "the Gossip Queen," would be detrimental. He promised in good faith to keep Skylar's secrets sealed, but money talks and in this case, his virtues were washed down the drain for lucrative tip of a $1000. Soon his fame in the world of hair would burn his reputation as "the Hair God."

What people like socialite Rose Highwater and famed hairstylist Arturo didn't realize was handsome billionaire Pierre Luca's name was not to be messed with. He had major ties to the most powerful people in the world, both good and bad. When it came to his reputation on the line and his family empire, the outcome could be more deadly than a *Page Six* story.

However, Pierre would shortly learn it was characters like Skylar that he could trust and have be part of his dark fantasy. Soon enough, Skylar's ever after fairytale drama would present itself in a magnificent Silver Invitation, giving her an exclusive invite into the secret society of the rich and famous, shifting *Hollywood Dreams* into a spotlight she never dreamed of. But first she would have to make her kitchen scenes exciting between her and Pierre Luca.

ACT II, SCENE 2
AN EVER AFTER DRAMA

INT: PIERRE LUCA'S KITCHEN

FADE IN

Pierre Luca warmly greets Skylar with a bouquet of white roses. She feels like she is in a fairytale. Skylar looks beautiful: her long blonde hair cascades past her boobs, her olive skin glows and her full lips are kissable as soon they would be sucking on hand-fed strawberries and champagne. Pierre puts the chocolate soufflé in the oven and then heads over to Skylar. He takes her hand tightly and leads her to the large glass dining table and she sits down. She is a bit nervous and Pierre pours her a glass of champagne and then one for himself. He raises his glass.

PIERRE LUCA: To ever after.

Skylar raises her glass and they toast, then he plants a passionate kiss.

PIERRE LUCA: It's not everyday I meet someone like you. I must say you took me for surprise.

SKYLAR: How so?

PIERRE LUCA: From the way you kissed me to the way you ran your hands through my hair, and our intimate conversation. I believe we have a deep connection and it's not every day that I invite someone to join me behind closed doors. You are the second woman to be invited from the club since I have been in the USA the past three years. I hope you are along for the adventure of an ever after.

SKYLAR: I'm ready.

PIERRE LUCA: First, get comfortable (*she takes off her jacket*) and make yourself at home. I just want you to be yourself and be open to my fantasies. They are a bit darker than vanilla. (*looks over toward the bedroom*) By the way do you like strawberries and whipped cream?

SKYLAR: I love strawberries and cream. Can I feed you one, baby?

PIERRE LUCA: Of course, but before you start feeding me, I want to go over some ground rules so we can ignite the "Ever After Drama" that is going to start once you address me as "Dark Knight." I call the shots here. From this moment on, I'm the dom and you are my sub, and soon enough you will be begging for my pleasure.

Skylar is shocked where the dialogue is going.

SKYLAR: Hmmm.

PIERRE LUCA: So, what do you say?

SKYLAR: Can I ask a question?

PIERRE LUCA: Sure.

SKYLAR: What does being your sub entail? Does that mean I have to be tied to the bed posts with handcuffs and ropes?

PIERRE LUCA: We may do that once or twice, but I assure you the outcome of everything I'm going to have you do is pleasure. You can say no at any time, but the more you trust me, the greater chances you have for a future with me. Do you trust me?

Skylar can't believe he is speaking about a future with the possibility of her being his girlfriend, not to mention what it will do to her career. Her life as a starving artist will be forever gone, transforming her into a real-life princess. This is stuff that only happens in Disney fairytales like Cinderella, not to small town girls named Skylar Lynn. She hesitates.

PIERRE LUCA: That's not convincing. I need your trust for this to work. Let's try it again. Do you trust me?

SKYLAR: I do.

PIERRE LUCA: Better. Right now, all I need from you tonight as my sub is to listen for the command "Dark Knight wants Princess to…" This is my command for the two of us behind closed doors only. It's not always going to be this exact command if I decide to extend you my Silver Invitation.

Skylar can't believe what she's hearing, yet is intrigued at the same time. She has heard about the culture of the sub and dom and read about role playing scenarios through her erotic novels, but never explored this avenue in any of her past relationships.

SKYLAR: Silver Invitation?

PIERRE LUCA: Yes, it's my invitation to my private world and the possibility of you becoming more than a sub. Maybe a girlfriend or, if you play your cards right, possibly my fiancé. I can be arm in arm with you on the red carpet at *the Golden Globes.*

All Skylar needs to hear is "Golden Globes," which confirms she and Pierre have a soul connection from another lifetime, too. She goes with her gut and decides to play by his rules. Her nervous energy turns into excitement, knowing they have a spiritual connection because he saw the dream she had for 25 years—herself as a Hollywood actress and writer at the Golden Globes.

SKYLAR: I'm in, but what if I just can't do something or want you to stop?

PIERRE LUCA: Then just say "vanilla." I'm going to keep it super light initially. Before you know it, you will be begging me to command you because the orgasms I will give you in my dark fantasy will be nothing like you ever experienced.

Skylar is in shock and really has no clue what is in store for her, except that she is in the Penthouse apartment of the world's youngest billionaire.

SKYLAR: I'm all yours, Dark Knight.

PIERRE LUCA: That's what I like to hear. First, Dark Knight wants princess to open the gift box and read the card out loud, then feed him chocolate-covered strawberries.

Skylar opens the greeting card and reads.

SKYLAR: "Naughty Princess, the Dark Knight is ready to torment, tease, and delight you in the most pleasurable ways. Your beautiful flesh will feel the touch of my masculinity, your ass will get slapped perfectly to show you who is in charge, your juicy lips will get kissed passionately to show you my desire and your orgasms will be extraordinary, so you stay my princess. I will excite you like no man has before. In the box, you will find a piece of sexy lingerie to slip into. There is another box awaiting you in my bathroom to open. You are to put on the lingerie, then come back and sit down near the champagne glasses so we start part one of the dark fantasy.

PIERRE LUCA: Princess, I will be waiting.

Skylar immediately takes the box back through his mater bedroom to his huge bathroom. The bathroom looks exactly like an editorial photo out of Home & Gardens magazine. The design has a French vintage theme with a crème marble stone design that only high-end designers with ultra rich clients could emulate. At the other end of the bathroom are French doors which open to a large, beautiful terrace balcony. Skylar doesn't want to open the doors, but she figures one day, maybe, she will get the chance.

The bathroom is around 700 square feet, fit for a king and queen. The shower area is huge—it could fit six people at once—and beautifully decorated with a charcoal grey marble interior to contrast the crème floors. It has the most advanced modern technology a shower could have: electronically activated with six shower heads, a built-in stereo and steam system. About 30 feet from the shower area is a huge Jacuzzi-style bath. It could fit up to four people and the color stone interior was the same grey marble as in the shower. The ceilings are high and from above hangs a vintage crystal chandelier. The front of the bathroom has three vanity sinks with crystal fixtures and a long rectangular mirror plastered above. The detail that went into the bathroom makes it eye-catching to anyone that walks in. Skylar feels as if she is in a style segment from Robin Leach's TV show, Lifestyles of the Rich and Famous.

She begins to shift her focus to the sexy lingerie—a red lace halter teddy with a low open back that ties in a bow around her lower back. At the end of the bathroom she notices a Manolo Blahniks box with a note card that reads, "To my Princess, welcome to my world." She just gets chills that moment and can feel her life and role in Hollywood Dreams about to change before her own eyes. Inside the box is an elegant pair of silver heels. Pierre did his research as any Dark Knight would and the size eight Manolo Blahniks fit her feet perfectly. Staring at herself in the mirror, she feels like a modern-day Cinderella. She no longer sees the life of an extra behind the scenes like she did in City of Dreams, but rather a sexy star ready to explode with passion in her most risqué role yet. She catches a second look at her new looks and is stunned how sexy she looks. Her looks just match her newfound attitude and all that was missing before she heads out to see her Dark Knight is her lip gloss. She takes out her pink lip gloss plumper and baby pink lip pencil. She goes slightly over her lip lines, creating a bigger lip, shading her real lip with the light pink pencil, and then takes the pink lip gloss plumper to make her lips look both *fuller and juicier. She then takes out the signature vanilla amber scent she created from the oils in her apartment and sprays some in the most erogenous zones: her neck, ears, chest, lower bikini area and inner thighs. She looks at herself one more time before making her appearance back in the kitchen and out of nowhere, a greater power comes over her, radiating from the Silver Heels, transforming her into a real life goddess for her upcoming scenes with Pierre.*

PIERRE LUCA: Dark Knight wants princess to come out and start feeding me.

Skylar quickly exits his large bathroom into the master bedroom, which is a showstopper, too. As she enters the kitchen, Pierre's heart begins to beat rapidly and for a moment, his fascination for the young Hollywood dreamer is real. He can feel the warmth of her beauty radiating from her soul, as the light from the Silver Heels began to spotlight the beginning of their Ever After Drama.

PIERRE LUCA: Wow... I'm a lucky man.

SKYLAR: Dark Knight, I have a naughty pleasure for you. Open your mouth wide. *(She begins to take the strawberries and feeds it to him in a sensual way)*

He begins to bite slowly as he is mesmerized with Skylar. He then reciprocates by feeding her a strawberry, except he dips the strawberry in whipped cream and then takes one finger with whipped cream and begins to spread some of the whipped cream on her neck. He feeds her the strawberries and then licks slowly where he placed the whipped cream. As he kisses her neck, he tugs the back of her long hair to let her know he is calling the shots and firmly brings her face closer to his as they start kissing passionately. Pierre grabs Skylar's hips and begins to massage her breasts over the lingerie. Skylar begins to feel the intense heat igniting between them and just like that, he pulls back and says, "I have a surprise, my princess."

He claps his hands and the music turns on. Of all songs, it's Stevie Wonder's "For Once in My Life." Pierre begins to lead her away from the dining room table toward the living room into performing a ball-room dance.

He begins to take her hand, and his feet shuffle into a rhumba, a slow, erotic Latin dance. She begins to make direct contact into his ocean blue eyes, as they begin to look at each other with undeniable lust. They begin dancing as if they've danced for years, clinging to one another. Skylar hyperextends her legs as Pierre twists her. She follows his lead as her hips move to the beats of music and his body of steel perfectly moves in sync with the swaying of her hips. Skylar feels the internal rhythm of their connection as the music begins to change beat and for a quick two seconds, she sees a flashback from the 1920s of her and Pierre dancing at a ballroom gala together. In her vision, she can see Republican party signs all around. Her vision fades quickly into reality as her mind goes back to following the natural rhythm of his body and her dance moves just mirror his. Their short dance confirms to Skylar that they have been dance partners before, and their meeting in this lifetime was not an accident but part of her fate. As the song ends, Pierre dips her down, then grabs her body closer to his and whispers.

PIERRE LUCA: It's always been you. The moment I saw you dance on stage.

Skylar's heart is beating so fast from the dance and the flashback. The déjà vu leaves her in somewhat of a trance. She feels like she is floating in and out of reality. Everything just seems to good to be true and the night is still young.

PIERRE LUCA: Now that you finished the first half of our date, the second half is going to be all about tasting temptation. Follow my instructions, Princess.

SKYLAR: Yes, Dark Knight.

PIERRE LUCA: Welcome to my Food Fantasy.

SKYLAR: It smells amazing.

PIERRE LUCA: I'm going to blindfold you first, and then tease you a bit before I feed you each one of my signature dishes. After I finish feeding you, you will have a chance to guess all the dishes and then, for grand finale of the night, if and only if you pass the last part of the night, a Silver Invitation will be waiting for you in my bathroom.

SKYLAR: A Silver Invitation. This seems like a fairytale.

PIERRE LUCA: It's our fairytale only if you keep obeying my commands. You cannot open the Silver Invitation until I give you the command. I'm going to just blindfold you first, so relax and let me do my magic.

Just when Skylar thinks her night is heading toward a classic, romantic date, it takes an interesting turn. She nods nervously but calms her anxiety by reminding herself that the supernatural force of the Silver Heels are protecting her and letting fate take its course by bringing Pierre to her. If Skylar plays her cards right, the Silver Invitation will open doors to his connections with agents and producers that will get Hollywood Dreams recognized by the Hollywood Press.

THE TASTE OF TEMPTATION

Soon enough, Skylar's hormones will be raging from his second part of the night, the Taste of Temptation. His prepared aphrodisiac dishes are infused with all the right flavors and ingredients that will incite her hormones to moan. His signature dishes will produce a surge of sexual energy that will overtake Skylar's hormones so much that by the time she enters the third part of the date, the master bedroom fantasy, she will be begging the Dark Knight to tear off his clothes and enter her insides.

Pierre takes the silver blindfold and gently wraps it around Skylar. He claps again, the music turns to Marvin Gaye's "Sexual Healing," and the upbeat music really hits Skylar that moment. Pierre goes to the kitchen to grab his three signature dishes that make girls like Skylar experience their first foodgasm. He is a professional romancer with expertise in aphrodisiac foods and he has his three dishes perfectly cooked and flavored in such a way that will overwhelm Skylar's sexual urges and she will be ready to go all the way in his bedroom.

He proceeds toward Skylar and lines up his three signature dishes in the following order: cherry ricotta crostini followed by seared scallops in a savory herb sauce, and a chocolate soufflé with his signature red wine chocolate glaze. He reaches for the flavorful martini he made with vodka and strawberry liquor, lime juice and some coconut sugar, garnished with a drizzle of chocolate glaze around the glass.

PIERRE LUCA: Princess, relax. I'm going to start with my signature drink called "Lust," which you will sip slowly and then swallow.

He brings the drink right up to her mouth and she sips it slowly, just as he commanded. Her face was beginning to blush as she was starting to enjoy herself.

SKYLAR: This is incredible.

PIERRE LUCA: It's not finished. (*He takes his finger and touches the chocolate drizzle so he can gather enough to feed Skylar*) Open up your mouth. I'm going to have you lick my finger.

Skylar begins to lick his finger and the combination of the straw-berries and the red wine chocolate glaze garnishing the martini cup creates a foodgasm. This flavor just sends her tastes and euphoric pleasure to another level of bliss. She has never tasted a martini drink so orgasmic.

SKYLAR: Oh my Godddd. (*loudly*)

PIERRE LUCA: Princess, the real fun begins. I have my first signature dish. I'm going to feed it to you. (*He grabs a small part of the spicy cherry crostini and gets ready to feed Skylar*). You can bite now, Princess, and remember to chew slowly.

Skylar begins to bite slowly and the flavor is savory yet sweet, with a bit of spiciness. She definitely can taste the flavor of both cherry and ricotta exploding in her mouth. The combination and the aftertaste of sweetness she just swallowed explodes with pleasure. Pierre is literally seducing her with his exquisite culinary skills. His food, thus far, verifies part of the stereotype that Skylar mentioned in City of Dreams—that French men are the best chefs. Soon enough she will verify the second part: they are the best lovers.

Pierre brings the martini to her mouth and gently helps her take a sip. Then he takes a little bit more of the red wine chocolate drizzle from the glass.

PIERRE LUCA: Open up, baby, I'm going to give you my finger to lick.

Skylar begins to lick his finger and something in the chocolate sauce is literally making her hormones rage. He removes his finger, then grabs her face and starts passionately kissing her, sucking her bottom lip in a way you only see in a soft porn movie. Then he tells her to relax for a minute before they finish the last two dishes. He starts kissing her neck and he can smell her amber vanilla scent, which gets his cock super hard. Skylar can feel how hard it is as he presses his body firmly against hers. He begins to kiss around her hair and neck, teasing her in such as way that she will scream once she tastes the chocolate soufflé. Then all of sudden, Rod Stewarts's song, "Do Ya Think I'm Sexy?" comes on, adding another level of temptation to the erotic date.

PIERRE LUCA: Please sip some of this drink before we go to the next dish.

Pierre brings the glass to Skylar's juicy lips and then she slowly sips. She is already starting to feel the effects of the alcohol as her body temperature is starting to rise. The food has really started to tap into her hormones and she can't believe the aphrodisiac food he cooked is turning her on in such a way that she is getting hot and bothered.

SKYLAR: I'm ready, Dark Knight.

PIERRE LUCA: Princess, I'm going to hold the surprise dish near your nose and I want you to smell it. Then I'm going to feed it to you. Open your mouth.

Pierre Luca begins to hold the shallot herb seared scallops near her nose. Skylar smells the aromatic flavor of the herbs, which add a different element to her foodgasm than the last dish.

PIERRE LUCA: Open your mouth, Princess, and keep chewing until I say the word "swallow."

Skylar takes a bite of the scallop and continues to chew for 15 seconds, and then she hears his command.

PIERRE LUCA: Swallow, Princess.

Skylar is amazed how much her mouth waters from the aromatic flavor of the herbs and how he calculated the precise order of his dishes to create an orgasmic experience. She begins to feel all warm and tingly inside.

SKYLAR: Oh my.

PIERRE LUCA: Just wait until you taste my dessert. I saved the best for last.

SKYLAR: Mi amore.

PIERRE LUCA: It's Dark Knight.

SKYLAR: Yes, Dark Knight.

PIERRE LUCA: You haven't tasted anything yet. Hold on.

Pierre gets up with the chocolate soufflé in hand and goes to his signature red wine chocolate glaze and fondue. He drizzles more of the warm rich sauce over the soufflé. He claps his hands and the music changes to "I'm on Fire" by Bruce Springsteen. Then he goes back to Skylar and slices a few of the strawberries next to him. He takes a generous spoonful with the sauce. The lyrics of the music are sensual with the words "desire" and "I'm on Fire" resonating with Skylar's tantric vibrations.

PIERRE LUCA: Princess, I'm going to feed you something juicy before we start my final dish. Open and wait for my command to swallow.

Skylar opens as he feeds her the sliced strawberries. She continues to chew for ten seconds until she hears his command.

PIERRE LUCA: Swallow.

Skylar needs a moment to compose herself between the sultry music, his body of steel and his woodsy, pheromone scent. Her hormones were raging so much, she was about to scream during her first foodgasm.

PIERRE LUCA: Let me know when you're ready for my signature dish.

SKYLAR: I'm ready, Dark Knight.

PIERRE LUCA: Open.

Pierre Luca begins to feed her a generous spoonful of his chocolate soufflé. Skylar is conditioned now to chew for 15 seconds, savoring the rich flavor of the dessert. She notices the texture is light and the flavor is decadent and rich. The soufflé is topped with the exotic red wine chocolate glaze which sends Skylar's "oh mys" to a high pitch. Right there and then, she experiences her first orgasm with food. The soufflé called the Chocolate Orgasm surges her dopamine levels to a new high and she began to scream out of nowhere.

SKYLAR: Oh My God! Oh, Dark Knight.

Pierre has one sliced strawberry in the chocolate glaze, waiting for Skylar to complete his signature dessert.

PIERRE LUCA: I have one more naughty bite before we play food trivia. I'm going to give you the name of the last dish. Since you're following my commands so well, you will only have to guess two of my dishes to go onto the next round. This is called the Chocolate Orgasm. Open slowly

Skylar begins to open her mouth again and just when she thinks her moaning was contained, the flavor of the chocolate glaze dipped in the strawberry just hits all the rights spots and she starts to have another foodgasm, stronger than the one before.

SKYLAR: Oh my fucking God! You are amazing (*she is high from the food and licks her lips*)

PIERRE LUCA: Princess, this is just the beginning. I'm going to put away the food and when I get back, I'm going to take your blindfold off and I want you to be quiet. First, relax and bend your head back a little. You have some chocolate on your lips.

Pierre takes a linen napkin and wipes Skylar's mouth delicately and then kisses her neck, teasing her with what is coming next. He hurries back to the chef's counter and put the dishes toward the back of the kitchen near the sink. He claps his hands once again and the music changes to Britney Spears' hit, "I'm a Slave 4 U." He goes to his armoire chest in his bedroom and gets out the vintage inspired crystal box which was fit for a queen. Inside the box is Skylar's Silver Invitation. He sets the box on the bathroom counter closest to the shower. Then he goes back toward the kitchen area where Skylar is sitting.

This will be the second invitation Pierre gives away during his three-year stay in the US. The other Silver Invitation was given to a girl named Angelica Marcello. Angelica was nothing like a fairytale character for the handsome Dark Knight. She didn't last more than a week as she didn't obey the Dark Knight's rules and had a huge drug problem. She was beautiful on the outside with looks like Sophia Loren, but her insides were torn apart. She was cold, catty, and a narcissist at heart who was just out for herself. On top of that, she couldn't play the role of his girlfriend when they were at high society events. She had no class or etiquette, starting fights with just about anyone. She was born into mafia roots and she was a hardcore Italian from Brooklyn. When she talked, it sounded like she was yelling and there was no filter on whatever she was thinking, she would just spew it! Pierre made sure she was no longer working in any New York City strip club business as he sent her a one-way ticket to Vegas with a paid apartment to get her out of his hair. She ended up marrying one of the biggest mobsters and drug lords out there, Carlos Sanchez, half brother to Levi Sanchez. It took about a month of damage control and half a million dollars in public relations and attorneys to clear his name with Angelica Marcello.

FADE OUT

Skylar really had no clue how her fairytale of the Ever After Drama was going to play out. She also had no clue just how powerful Pierre Luca really was, but she would later learn this young man was not to be messed with. At the flip of a switch, he had the power to make all her dreams come true or destroy her dreams to pieces, pausing her dialogue and any *Page Six* stories that would recognize *Hollywood Dreams*. In spite of Pierre Luca's controlling ways, he saw Skylar was different from the other dancers and girls he dated. He was ready to explore their relationship of Dark Knight and Princess. He truly loved Skylar's free-spirited personality, down to earth attitude and unconventional ways that it made it impossible for him not to grant her a Silver Invitation, no matter if she didn't correctly guess the dishes. In his head she already passed his food trivia, but he still had to heighten the suspense.

Skylar had no clue what dialogue and cues were next in her scenes, but all she knew was how hot and bothered she became from his orgasmic food. She couldn't get the taste of the chocolate-covered strawberries and *the Chocolate Orgasm* out of her head. Soon enough, her food fantasies would be fading into a wetter adventure awaiting her in his fantasy bathroom. All Skylar needed to do was keep playing the role of the submissive princess well, so the Dark Knight would keep her around much longer than his first submissive, Angelica Marcello.

CHAPTER 8
THE SMELL OF A RAT

No one likes the smell of a rat, especially when the smell becomes intolerable, leaving only one solution: extermination. In the world of the mob and Wall Street, extermination happens quite frequently. Although Wall Street and the mob are two different animals entirely, they practically butt heads. When they discover a rat, the dialogue becomes volatile, vulgar and even dangerous.

John Marino, a top Wall Street executive, was still in rage and sniffing out the streets of New York City to find the rat who turned his life around. Meanwhile, the drama from Wall Street was starting to storm into the underground world of Silver Lights where the storylines were getting a new twist.

Tony Murano, managing director and part owner at Silver Lights, also known as "the Lion King" would receive the horrible news. He lived up to his nickname because of the way he executed power. When there was a problem, he roared to restore order, so his voice would be heard across Silver Lights. A middle-aged man from Brooklyn with Italian roots in the mafia. He was on the taller side for being Italian, standing at six feet two. His body resembled a bodyguard while his face looked like the iconic Mr. Clean. He turned a blind eye to the Wall Street and political scandals over the years, thinking that his home, Silver Lights, would be immune, but boy, was he wrong. Tony's deep roots within the mafia would prove his reputation as "the Lion King." The dangerous scandal taking place right under his nose was just about to spotlight the seedy world of organized crime.

20 years of experience in the adult entertainment industry made Tony unbreakable when it came to protecting his club. Tony was dealing with a few small fires after Skylar came on board. One of them being the possibility of Gemstone Hospitality not investing, and the worst one coming out of nowhere, money laundering.

EARLY YEARS OF HIS MAFIA ROOTS

Tony learned as a young kid, if it didn't concern your family, then don't stick you nose where it didn't belong. Growing up in the streets among the Grecos, New York's largest organized crime family in the 80s, made him grow up real fast and taught him early on not to trust anyone, not even his own blood. He became acquainted at an early age with the world of the mafia. Throughout his teens, he worked as busboy in the Italian joint, Rosalina's. From the outside world, it looked like a traditional Italian restaurant, but from the inside, it looked more like a behind-the-scenes operations from *Goodfellas*. Everything illegal was taking place: gambling, drugs, hookers and laundering. The mafia would come in daily and use Rosalina's to plot out their hit list, and what capos (*heads of business*) they were going to appoint in charge of the different crimes. A weekly agenda included their target list of converting cops, vandalism on businesses that weren't coming aboard, and strategies to expanding their drug cartel and money laundering business. A normal Sunday dinner typically looked like a few shootings, packages of blow being smuggled, and disposal of dead bodies.

The main ringleader at the time was the Greco Family before the Marzianos took reign. Nicholas Greco, "the Shark," was head of operations and his son Nicholas, Jr., worked with Tony at the restaurant. Dominick Santorini and Tommy D were head capos and were still part of the current organized crime family of the Marzianos. As Tony worked his way up in the kitchen of Rosalina's, he would learn the dialogue of the mob and their honor code.

ACT II, SCENE III
GOODFELLAS

FADE IN

1980s ROSALINA'S in BROOKLYN

Tony is clearing plates from the back room where the capos are conducting their business and plotting local crime of tax evasion, money laundering, and drug racketeering. It's just like a scene out of the famous movie Goodfellas.

NICHOLAS GRECO, SR.: We have 10 kilos of cocaine that need to be moved from Rosalina's tomorrow and delivered to the Pizzeria. Who is doing that?

DOMINICK SANTORINI: I will.

NICHOLAS GRECO, SR.: Next round of business is the Bensonhurst Police unit. Do we have any new converts?

TOMMY D: Robert Felder is questionable. I followed him the other day and cornered him in the alley. He gave me his verbal word he is in.

NICHOLAS GRECO, SR.: That's not good enough. We had a past issue with him almost ratting on the money laundering in Billy's dry cleaning shop. You need to slash his tires tomorrow to let him know that this is his last warning and follow up with a night visit. This should make him scared shitless.

Tony Murano isn't surprised about the conversation happening, and is minding his own business like usual, however Nicholas, Jr. happens to interrupt.

NICHOLAS GRECO, JR.: Pops, I heard the city council is having a meeting tomorrow about the dead bodies that have been popping up in sanitation.

NICHOLAS GRECO, SR.: I'm aware, Junior. I will notify Vinny Marcello, Sr., he owns the biggest sanitation business in Brooklyn, and has our back. He has been helping us dispose the weekly bodies. We are one step ahead of that pathetic City Council. They think they make rules but it's the other way around. The Grecos make all the rules.

NICHOLAS GRECO, JR.: Good to know, Pops. (*gives him a hug*)

NICHOLAS GRECO, SR.: Finish cleaning up and get back home. Your mother needs your help around the house.

Nicholas, Jr. nods and quickly gathers the rest of the dirty dishes.

TOMMY D: Don't worry, boss, I will make sure Sergeant Robert Felder is on board tomorrow and I will also make a night call for jewelry.

NICHOLAS GRECO, JR.: Tony, are you listening to this?

TONY: I'm not listening, sir, just trying to get the dishes to the kitchen.

NICHOLAS GRECO, SR.: Kid, come here... Listen up, because one day you may find yourself in trouble and you won't have anyone to bail your ass out. If you listen more to our meetings, you will gain something money can't buy: knowledge. Without knowledge you don't have power. Knowledge is the difference between a leader over a follower. You hear me? The reason you are working for us is that you are meant to become a leader.

TONY: I hear you loud and clear, sir.

NICHOLAS GRECO, SR.: You must always have the knowledge to think two steps ahead of your enemy. I see the way you work, your loyalty and hard work, so start listening. Capisce?

TONY: Capisce.

TOMMY D: Now on to matters of Wall Street. The biggest thing going on is the stock scam that is happening with Franco Matthews. The New York Stock Exchange has been running an investigation the past few days and Franco reached out yesterday for our help with laundering the money he has for selling fake stocks. He has around $500,000 from the past quarter and he said we could get a 50% cut if we could help him hide the money. I think Francesca's Bakery would be the place.

NICHOLAS SENIOR: I agree. Its catering business makes a perfect disguise so the Feds would never think to look there.

FADE OUT

The conversation with Nicholas Greco, Sr. that day in the 1980s left quite an impression on Tony, one he never forgot and would take him to his starring role in *Hollywood Dreams*. He took the advice to not trust anyone, to keep his mouth shut and to look someone dead in the eyes to see if they were telling the truth. He also started viewing himself as a future leader, and one day he would be managing a business too.

Tony quickly grew accustomed to the weekly meetings and even started participating in some of their activities, delivering packages of illegal drugs and aiding in money laundering, until the Feds raided Rosalina's when he was 17 years old. Nicholas, Sr. and the top 20 capos at the time received a lengthy sentence in the slammer—27 to 28 years with possibility of parole. There were a few rats and undercover cops that got a shorter jail sentence than Nicholas Sr., and his cronies, Tommy D and Dominick Santorini. Luckily, since Tony was a juvenile at the time and there was no direct evidence linking him to their charges, he was cleared 100%, giving him a chance to break free from a life of organized crime.

Shortly after the Grecos got locked up, the Marziano family was next in line to take their place and from that day on and into the current feature, *Hollywood Dreams*, the Marzianos ran all operations over the five boroughs. Rumors were circulating in Brooklyn that Nicholas, Sr. was to be released in the late winter to early spring of 2015. Tommy D, and Dominick Santorini got out earlier, in 2013, because of lesser charges and cooperation with the Feds. To their luck, they were offered lower positions with the Marziano Family, however, the Marzianos didn't know Tommy D and Dominick were secretly plotting to take over the head of the New York City mafia once "the Shark" was released. If for some reason, Nicholas, Sr. got an early release date before the blow up of the Louis Mazarati scandal and the feuding rivalry between Onyx Equities and Sapphire Investments, then all hell would break loose between the Grecos and The Marzianos in *Hollywood Dreams*. In the world of the mafia, betrayal only meant one thing: dead bodies and a big payday, one that could affect the whole entire political and economic landscape of New York.

After the lock up of the Grecos, Tony left his dealings with the mob at Rosalina's. He continued to move forward on a path void of crime, moving up the ranks of the hospitality industry from bar back to manager, to his first career break as the head manager and part owner of Silver Lights. In the back of his head, that conversation with Nicholas, Sr. in the 1980s never left his mind. It resonated strongly in all his business decisions and shaped the strong businessman he became, moving up the ranks in a short period of time as a leading businessman in the world of adult entertainment. Tony would soon have his chance to rekindle old conversations with his former mentor Nicholas, Sr., who was about to be released from prison amidst New York City's biggest Ponzi scam, the Louis Mazarati scam. Tony would randomly bump into his former friend, Nicholas, Jr., a few days before the Silver Lights masquerade party. If Nicholas, Jr. remembered Tony's honorable character, a big favor from the Grecos would be the lifeline Tony desperately needed to keep from going bankrupt or worse, going behind bars. However, no favor was free with the mob, and there would be a price he would have to pay in return.

BACK TO THE LOUIS MAZARATI RUMORS

Tony couldn't believe the rumors were actually true that Louis Mazarati's firm, Emerald Investments, was being charged on several counts by the FBI. The whole firm, along with 30 outsiders, were facing charges of tax evasion, fraud, conspiracy, money laundering, and the list goes on.

Initially, Tony wasn't worried because he thought there would be no way in a million years him or someone from his club would have any direct association with the scam. The possibility of someone working for him using Silver Lights to launder and embezzle money would soon turn Tony's world upside down.

Tony glanced at the latest headlines from the New York Post, "Ponzi Scam Affects Big Apple." He browsed the article and it mentioned a quote from Whitmore Reynolds, president of the New York Stock Exchange, discussing the severity of the charges. Just as Tony read the quote, his phone got a text from Donald Singer, vice president at Louis Mazarati's firm and co-founder of Emerald Investments.

Donald's text read, "Tony, I just wanted to give you a heads-up so you're prepared when the FBI contacts you. They raided our firm today and all records, contacts, accounts and contracts are in the FBI hands. I don't want to say more as I'm not sure if my phone is being tapped. Have a good day and I hope to see you next week at our spot."

Tony was shocked at what he was reading. He knew whenever there were Wall Street scandals or white-collar crimes being committed, the first places the Feds searched were be the local gentlemen's clubs. He was quite familiar with these scenarios, however he was caught off guard by Donald Singer's text, as he wasn't mentally prepared for the fireworks that were going to explode before his eyes. Part of him wanted to reach out to Donald Singer and Rodger Matthews of Emerald Investments, and ask more questions, but Tony knew better it was best to let things unravel, so he would just wait.

How could Tony be in the dark for two years with money laundering going down in his own club and his company being associated to one of the biggest scandals of all time? Tony had no clue who would betray the honor code of Silver Lights. He couldn't even think that his own employees would do something like this. He looked at his employees like family, including Redmond, Michael Donahue, and Frankie Martinez. Another suspect in question was financial controller and counsel Blake Stevens, but what would be his motive? The last suspects were a few vendors they worked with: Eddie Maggio of New York Security Confidential and Joey Henderson of Data Integrations. Both had access to all Silver Lights' sales and data information from the POS system. Last but not least was Travis Key, vice president and head contact for their merchant system vendor, American Freedom, which was the POS that they used to run all credit cards and debits cards in the club.

Tony had his hands full hunting down all the suspects in question. It would be in the final acts that there would be a startling discovery that would bring back Tony's past to the present, shaking up the FBI scandal. One thing that was certain in *Hollywood Dreams*: a big payday was coming.

ACT II, SCENE IV
PAYDAY IS COMING

FADE IN

INT: SILVER LIGHTS BACK OFFICE

Time Period: one week before the Masquerade Ball

Tony's anxiety about the Louis Mazarati Ponzi Scam and the Wall Street news of insider trading is starting to consume him. This is definitely affecting Silver Lights' business and the future. His phone is ringing with an incoming call which the caller id traces to THE FEDERAL BUREAU OF INVESTIGATION (FBI).

DIALOGUE

FBI INFORMANT FRANK: Is this Tony Murano?

TONY MURANO: Speaking. Who is this?

FBI INFORMANT FRANK: Frank Piazza from the FBI. I'm calling in regards to Louis Mazarati's firm.

TONY MURANO: How can I help you, sir?

FBI INFORMANT FRANK: Please, call me Frank.

TONY MURANO: OK, Frank, what is this about?

FBI INFORMANT FRANK: I'm going to cut straight to the chase. Your company, Diamond Hospitality, is in question with regards to the Louis Mazarati scandal. Recent findings have been brought to our attention, pointing to your firm as a possible suspect in this scam.

TONY MURANO: How in the world would we be a suspect? We have no direct dealings with their firm.

FBI INFORMANT FRANK: Well, that's not what our identified source says. Your club is on the verge of being charged with money laundering and embezzling.

Tony's heart skips a beat, the sweat on his bald head begins to drip and his hands start to shake. He is starting to get angry and he responds back.

TONY MURANO: This is absolute nonsense! I watch this club like a hawk, and nothing like laundering would ever slip by me.

FBI INFORMANT FRANK: Mr. Murano, I have been doing this for 20 years, and you would be surprised how super easy money laundering and embezzling is to hide if someone has access to back operations and financials.

TONY MURANO: Can I ask you something Frank?

FBI INFORMANT FRANK: Yes.

TONY MURANO: What evidence do you have?

FBI INFORMANT FRANK: I'm not able to disclose the evidence right now. I was told to inform you that a week from Monday, we will have a warrant to search the club and go through any surveillance footage, financials, contracts, investor relations and employee information. You have the right to an attorney, and if you have any other questions or need to bring up anything to your defense you have my number.

The door to Tony's office is slightly open and there is a soft knock at the door. Standing outside the door is Redmond, second in charge at Silver Lights. Redmond's looks just make you do a second take. Often referred to as the countryman in Hollywood Dreams, he is definitely a fan favorite among all dancers and female customers. One can't help but notice how strikingly attractive he is. A clone to the famous hunky movie star, Charlie Hunnam, with piercing blue eyes that match his to-die-for southern accent and masculine body.

The sweet South Carolina gentleman will soon be faced with two entrances, one opening to faith and the other opening to greed. The door of faith will open up the possibility of becoming partner in Diamond Hospitality, working alongside "the Lion King," Tony Murano. The second door will open to a guaranteed life of greed with endless money, working alongside Wall Street's villains, Michael Donahue and Brooks Kennedy. Redmond will learn later that when one door closes, the other opens, and one of these doors will forever change his role in Skylar's third feature, Golden Dreams.

Redmond peeks in the office and realizes Tony is on the phone. Tony signals him to come in.

TONY MURANO: I'm going to reach out to my attorney, Pierce Mahoney, and if something comes up, I will have him reach out.

The phone clicks, and the receiver hangs up. Redmond is coming to Tony with good news that Silver Lights' biggest competitor, Penthouse, is running a drug cartel behind the scenes. The news couldn't come at a better time with the Feds about to raid Silver Lights next week for money laundering for the Louis Mazarati firm. This can be the lifeline that Silver Lights needs in saving their establishment from getting shut down. Redmond isn't supposed to say anything until they have their "Dirty Martini Special" meeting, which is code for "Operation Penthouse." This meeting is intended to protect their conspiracy and to avoid leaking information to outsiders. If anyone on the outside knows what they are doing, they could be faced with serious charges for corporate espionage.

REDMOND: T, is everything OK? You look like you just saw a ghost.

TONY: No, I have some horrible news. I just got off the phone with the FBI. A man by the name of Frank Piazza, who is the lead FBI agent on the Louis Mazarati case, said they have a source of evidence that directly links us to the charges with the scam.

REDMOND: What in the world are you talking about?

TONY: Red, someone from our company or a third party we do business with, has been laundering money through the back-door operations of Silver Lights. This is high priority, and if it's not resolved we can get shut down or worse, go to prison.

REDMOND: Don't even go there. I would never.

TONY: Let me finish. It's obvious we have a crook in a disguise who is one hell of an actor! My gut says to investigate the employees first, however the person who did this assumes we would do that first. So instead of searching our employees, I suggest we look toward outside suspects like our competitors, vendors and political figures that would have a motive in taking us down. If not one good lead comes up from the outside, then circle back to the club, including yourself. (*sarcastically*)

REDMOND: I'm still a countryman at heart from South Carolina if you haven't forgotten.

TONY: Well countrymen do hunt for the kill!

REDMOND: Indeed they do! They are messing with the wrong hunter. You know Silver Lights has been the only place I can call home in the Big Apple. T, I would never betray you after you took me under your wing when I had only ten dollars in my pocket and nothing else to my name. Not to mention you taught me everything I know about running a successful club. I wouldn't be half the man I am today. Do not underestimate my loyalty.

TONY: I'm not, but if you were in my shoes, you would have to look at everyone as a suspect to catch the crook.

REDMOND: Understood.

TONY: First things first. Start by contacting the financial controller, Blake Stevens, to find out if anyone else has had full access to our documents besides me. Next, contact our third-party vendors including Eddie Maggio, Travis Keys and Joey Henderson. Find out if there has been a breach of data among any of these vendors. The last area to search would be Penthouse. Find out if their top three customers compare to our top three customers. Remember the names Stefano Marcello and Angelo Bianchi, because they are Penthouse owners and have mob affiliations.

REDMOND: The place where Barbie works?

TONY: No shit, Sherlock! Competition in this business is dangerous and can possibly turn deadly if we don't play our cards right.

REDMOND: I'm in the game and I'm going to kill it!

TONY: Good, because you need to be two steps ahead of the criminal always, as my old mentor, Nicholas Greco, would say. Make sure you get to the financials today on Stefano Marcello and Angelo Bianchi and their top customers. I have a hunch they may have something to do with this. I will also let Barbie know what's going on so she can snoop around their office.

REDMOND: "The Shark" was your mentor?

TONY: Yes, he was, but that's a story for another time. Let's get on top of this.

Barbie is a beautiful blonde from South Carolina, who is Redmond's hometown sweetheart. They moved to the Big Apple together four years after high school, saving up from local jobs in their town over the years, and they both ended up finding work at Silver Lights. Barbie as a premiere exotic entertainer for five years and Redmond moving up the ranks to an assistant manager position.

Barbie left Silver Lights in Skylar's first feature, City of Dreams, under the pretense that Redmond was cheating. Their relationship hit an all-time low when she found out the rumors of Redmond's affair were all over the club. The worst part was the other woman was Amber Ray, New York City's hottest porn star, although Redmond denied it. Barbie decided to pack her bags and say good-bye, leaving her no choice but to work for their competitor, Penthouse. Prior to Barbie's exit, Tony approached her with a lucrative opportunity to work for Silver Lights as undercover spy at Penthouse, still allowing her to earn money as a dancer at Penthouse. The opportunity had a huge upside for Barbie because the more information she gathered on Penthouse, the fatter her bank account became.

REDMOND: I'm on top of it, T. There will be a big payday coming their way!

TONY: The payday will come only if you follow my instructions. Also, don't forget when you talk to Eddie Maggio, ask if he has seen anything in the footage over the past few months that would raise a red flag.

REDMOND: I will do that, but I initially came here to be the bearer of good news.

TONY: What is that?

REDMOND: It relates to the "Dirty Martini Special"

TONY: Please hold off on discussing matters until Sunday.

REDMOND: Well Barbie found a drug ring

TONY: Shh. Don't say any more. You never know if someone has tapped this place. I will let you know the location of the meeting on Sunday, and we can discuss then.

REDMOND: I thought you would be the first to jump at this information. The man heading the drug cartel is Ron Colombo, and he is one of the lead capos under the Marzianos.

TONY: Listen up, we are getting searched on Monday, and everything we say, do, or discuss needs to be monitored.

REDMOND: Understood, but I don't think you understand it's getting pretty heated every night for Barbie. Their main champagne host, Luke Matthews, is connected with the mob, taking packages of coke into the club. I'm talking fifteen kilos of coke every month are being laundered and then distributed to customers. She has been witnessing some of the heaviest hitters come into those rooms, from the mayor's right-hand man, councilman Terry Bianchi, who is also cousin to Angelo Bianchi of Penthouse. She says there are bags of blow in just about in every room you go into.

TONY: Really, and no Pos (*police*) have been there?

REDMOND: No, not yet, because they have a few crooked cops who are being paid off in the drug ring.

TONY: I'm going to look into this. I will reach out to Barbie shortly, and I will let you know if the meeting is going to be moved up, but first you have to play detective.

REDMOND: I will do that and move mountains for a big payday!

Tony looks down at his phone. He is getting text with a photo from Barbie: two men wearing suits talking outside the back entrance of Penthouse. One guy is standing close to a limo and the taller guy is in a suit. The taller guy is Brooks Kennedy, and the smaller guy appears a mystery. Barbie sends another photo with the caption "Brooks Kennedy" and "Ron Colombo." Tony texts back, "Keep this on the down low." Tony then looks up expressionless.

REDMOND: Is everything ok?

TONY: Everything is amazing, it's a text from Victoria. She says it's going to be a bit longer until she moves out because her new apartment won't be ready for another 8 days.

REDMOND: That sucks. When she is out, we should celebrate.

TONY: The celebration will be after we finish Operation Payday.

The message "Payday" was picked up by the high-tech secret cameras and security system in the club, secretly placed by Eddie Maggio under Michael Donahue's orders. The footage of the conversation that just took place was captured by the camera as a high priority alert, automatically sending alerts to Michael, Eddie and the bar back, Gus, to view the footage.

Luckily, Michael was already swinging big in the underground world of Wall Street, but one thing that could possibly mess up the rhythm of his swing would be airing his dirty laundry. Brooks Kennedy was also no stranger to secrets as his greed for monopolizing the financial markets blurred any possibility for redemption. Soon, enough one of these dirty secrets would start rotting so badly that the countryman, Redmond, would have no choice but to possibly burn them.

FADE OUT

With Silver Lights on the brink of being shut down and the smell of dirty secrets starting to rot away inside the club of Silver Lights, both Tony and Redmond would have to work smarter than ever. They would need to start interrogating Eddie Maggio and Michael Donahue, but if they were really good at playing detective, they would skip to the chase and start their interrogation with the hard working bar back named Gus, who would later be one of the bombshells blowing up the drama of *Hollywood Dreams*.

CHAPTER 9

THE VILLAINS OF WALL STREET

The scandals of Wall Street were at a new high in *Hollywood Dreams*, with the Villains of Wall Street starting to feel the heat. The stock exchange was at an ultimate high but behind the scenes, the Louis Mazarati scam was taking over the boiler room. Mayor Thomas Mahoney's political campaign for 2020 was about to fall apart, as he was illegally using government funds to secure donors and his biggest supporter, the Kennedy family, was about to feel that.

At the heart of every storyline, there is an antagonist and in *Hollywood Dreams*, there was more than one. These guys were referred to as the Villains of Wall Street and they were: Michael Donahue, Brooks Kennedy and "the Beast of Wall Street," Charles Marziano.

Unlike "the Beast," Michael Donahue was a leading player behind the scenes. A former white-collar criminal in charge of pushing all the champagne rooms and managing part of the operations at Silver Lights, he was as sharp as razor. If you messed with his deals, he would cut you fast. His skills as a former white-collar criminal and Wall Street trader worked to his advantage as he dealt with the mob and high-powered Wall Street executives in the world of Silver Lights.

Michael was on his way back to life of a Wall Street trader, except this time, it was behind the scenes at Silver Lights. Besides the spy cameras that hooked him back into the world of Wall Street, he made it his sovereign duty to become chummy with every big swinging dick that walked through the doors of Silver Lights, especially the ones he knew he could kiss ass and lure into giving him back pieces of his former life. One of these suckers happened to be socialite and financier Brooks Kennedy, owner of Onyx Equities.

In the *City of Dreams*, Brooks made Michael a lucrative offer he couldn't resist, which entailed Michael working as a financial consultant behind the scenes for his firm, without his name ever coming out on the books, while still maintaining his position at Silver Lights as senior champagne host. The only people who knew about Michael's private role at Onyx Equities were of course, Brooks and his financial controller, Ted Connors. Everything was practically hidden from the public, but if someone were to dig deep enough, they would catch the Wall Street Villains' secret job on the books, with a series of quarterly deposits spread out, equaling his $400,000 salary in addition to bonuses.

The more confidential, Wall Street information Michael received from the cameras, the higher the payouts. A series of $150,000 in quarterly bonuses came in and soon Michael was no longer living in a dumpy one-bedroom apartment, but rather a high-end brownstone. Michael kept his new lifestyle quiet in the club, however outside the club, his lavish toys flashed wealth, from his fully loaded 2015 Range Rover and $50,000 gold Rolex, to an automated smart town house in Brooklyn. It was just a matter of time before his flashy lifestyle on the outside would catch up to the inside world of Silver Lights, as the investigation would take a dramatic turn no one was expecting.

MICHAEL DONAHUE CONTINUES TO SPOTLIGHT DRAMA

Michael was no longer living a life of virtue, but rather of sin, turning his back on his faith and recovery, and cheating on his wife, Grace. He just became more corrupt in his scenes, exploiting many of the deals that were brewing up and having after-hours sex with his long-time mistress, Lola, "the Queen Bee." Lola, a top entertainer at Silver Lights, was the ideal dancer, keeping customers happy all night with her authority and leadership amongst the dancers. Her vivacious personality, Lucy Liu looks and appetite for fetish attracted Michael. They had after-hours sex in just about every place in the club, and quickies in his car, where she screamed louder than the bustling streets. Lola wasn't oblivious to what was going on, but she preferred to let things be, as her feelings of love were starting to blur her morals, overlooking Michael's bad boy ways.

In the end, Michael would benefit from telling Lola what he was doing, because the two could team up together. She could double his leads and be his ally in case all hell broke loose. It wouldn't be until the last act that he would possibly need her help. Michael knew he was violating the laws of the security exchange and creating an unfair monopoly amongst Wall Street firms, but what Michael didn't take into consideration was many of these under-the-radar deals and insider information he was providing to Brooks Kennedy were directly eating away at both the New York Stock Exchange and the American economy.

Michael's greedy appetite for money and power was on the brink of taking a deadly turn with consequences fatal enough that he could end up in the ground if he wasn't smart. It only took one slip-up for the white-collar criminal to be back in prison or caught amongst the wildfires of New York's biggest crime family, the Marzianos, where weekly morgue visits were a regular occurrence.

THE CORE DRAMA OF THE MARZIANO NAME

The Marzianos were not a family to mess with and their roots traced all the way back to the early 1900s, when the Grecos had power. When it came to who was in power with the mafia, there was no such thing as luck. It was all about dictatorship. The Marzianos planned their hit on the Grecos in the 1980s because the Grecos had absolute power. The hit was pulled off by a crooked federal agent by the name of Greg Sanders and a head capo by the name of Stephano Marcello, along with an anonymous politician and ally to the powerful Marziano brothers, Alfredo and Luigi. Alfredo was referred to as "the Godfather" of the entire New York Mafia. Luigi managed the capos, holding weekly borough meetings and coordinating organized crime. On occasion, the Marzianos were known to play with the best of Wall Street. When financial scandals broke, they looked for ways they could launder money, lend money or mitigate the damage by getting their crooked cops or higher up capos involved. It was a no brainer that soon enough, Michael's path would be coinciding head-on with the mob's, and soon their Sunday night dinners would entail a soup of blood and a feast of dead bodies.

Last but not least, the most important Villain of Wall Street was Charles Marziano, "the Beast of Wall Street." While he had the same last name as the mob family, he maintained his claim that he had no blood relation or affiliations with the Marzianos. Ironically, he looked and acted like Robert De Niro from *The Irishman*. He was 100% Italian and grew up on the streets of Brooklyn, where the mob ran his neighborhood. The black sheep, he took a different route than his peers by attending college, graduating magna cum laude, then continuing his education to receive an MBA at Wharton. He worked his way up the Wall Street ladder to managing and owning one of the largest firms on the exchange, Sapphire Investments. Under his fine, tailored Italian suits, he still had all the characteristics of a mobster, but he preferred to prevail over his mob-like tactics on the exchange by practicing tax evasion, blackmailing, stealing insider information and creating illegal monopolies.

His tactics worked for a decade until the day his firm got caught in one of their own scandals. It was his top dog, John Marino, senior managing director, who got caught in the act with insider trading. Unfortunately, he had no choice but to forfeit the possible merger between Precision Instruments and Sapphire Investments, along with millions of dollars to cover up their violation of trying to use insider information to create an unfair monopoly.

After the outcome of Precision Instruments, the fate of Sapphire Investments never looked quite the same. It was bleak in the corporate climate at Sapphire Investments, leaving the Beast with no option but to demote John Marino. In some regards, John was still the right wingman to the Beast, working closely with him all the time. Each day just got worse as the Beast's roller coaster of emotions just mirrored the highs and lows of the stock market. The more money the firm lost as the stock market hit a low, the more out of control the Beast became.

John Marino was in over his head and he needed a quick option to salvage the the hit his firm took from the Precision Instruments fiasco. If he couldn't find the next profitable, under-the-radar company to take public as an IPO (initial public offering) in the next few weeks, his job would soon be non-existent. However, five weeks later, he found out Camden Roberts (who gave John the insider information about Precision Instruments) was working for a different financial firm as a research analyst. This time, Camden texted John about a promising pharmaceutical company by the name of Vital Pharmaceuticals, and another company called Randall Pharmaceuticals, owned by Pierre Luca. Randall Pharmaceuticals was about to shake up the stock market with projections anticipated to double in shareholder stock once their big cancer drug hit the market. If Sapphire Investments could acquire a large percentage of Randall stocks before the drug entered the market, they could be back on the map as a leader. The smaller company, Vital Pharmaceuticals, managed and run by Grant Lawrence, also had a lot of potential, as they were on the cutting edge for developing drugs that decreased the symptoms of neurological disorders like muscular dystrophy and Parkinson's disease.

John already knew Philip Delfonte was working on this lead, but not closed it yet. John wasn't aware his nemesis, Onyx Equities, was also trying to take Vital Pharmaceuticals public winning over Grant Lawrence with a fun night in the champagne room. Pierre Luca's healthcare company was about to go public with the first immunotherapy drug for cancer patients that could be treated on kids too. If the drug worked as successfully as it did in the clinical trials, John knew this could possibly be his ticket out of the company doghouse and back into his former life of luxury.

He was on a mission in his upcoming meeting with "the Beast of Wall Street" to present this lead and convince Charles to advance some funding to Vital Pharmaceuticals. John was anxiously waiting outside Charles' office to be summoned for his weekly meeting with the Beast, and finally he heard his name called.

ACT II, SCENE V
CHEERS TO THE KING OF WALL STREET

FADE IN

INT: THE BEAST OF WALL STREET'S OFFICE

John walks confidently into the largest office of the floor, belonging to the Beast of Wall Street. The TV screens with the stock exchange numbers are plastered on the wall facing Charles. Along the opposite side wall closest to his desk is a bookcase display of family pictures portraying his Italian heritage, including black and white pictures from his days in Brooklyn, his daughter's baptism, and one of his fourth wife, Katherine May, a southern belle and transplant to New York City. The office is pristine clean and there are a few pieces of high-end art. John reminds himself to be calm and nonreactive no matter how angry Charles becomes. John never knows what scenario he is walking into because Charles' erratic moods mimic the weather forecast: one minute he's high-fiving John and the next he's chewing him out for bad business deals. Today is like any typical day with the scent of whiskey filling the room and John is ready to discuss the possibility of obtaining both Randall Pharmaceuticals and Vital Pharmaceuticals.

DIALOGUE

CHARLES MARZIANO: Do you want some? (*looking to the bottle of whiskey*).

JOHN MARINO: I will take some of that tequila.

Charles proceeds to make a drink with the tequila while discussing the numbers of the day.

CHARLES MARZIANO: Numbers are shooting in the energy sectors. The solar company, Sunshine Alternative Energy, keeps doubling. I want you to arrange meeting with the senior director for the east coast. Her name is Francesca Ferrari. (*hands the drink to John*)

John takes a sip.

JOHN MARINO: You really know how to make one hell of a drink. I think you are in the wrong profession.

CHARLES MARZIANO: Done with those days. I used to work as a bartender at Rosalina's in college. Let's get to business on Francesca Ferrari.

When John hears "Rosalina's," it just confirms his suspicions about Charles' ties to the mob. Rosalina's was a well-known mob joint for the Marziano family.

JOHN MARINO: Is she any relation to the Ferrari family?

CHARLES MARZIANO: That would be impossible, otherwise she would be working for the car company.

JOHN MARINO: Nothing is impossible. She does have the same last name so it's a possibility she could be related. I think it could be worth looking into before we set up a meeting.

CHARLES MARZIANO: Do that and see what else you can dig up. I have heard from a few of her male customers that once Francesca hits the tequila, she gets a bit wild, which could work in your favor.

JOHN MARINO: A woman that drinks tequila is a woman that has distinct tastes. This could be one hell of a night of business.

CHARLES MARZIANO: Don't let that fool you, because she brings another person with her, usually another male from her company. Sometimes she brings Henry Romano, the president, or just an employee, but she won't give you a heads up. Whoever she brings will just show up unannounced. Marino, if you some how bring their company on board with his stamp of approval then your life here on will be much different.

The spit coming out of the Beast's mouth just intensifies how impor-tant it is to bring Henry Romano on board and secure the biggest energy deal of the century. Charles is intoxicated, but proficient in what he is saying. John agrees and is ready to discuss the possible merger of Randall Pharmaceuticals. Henry Romano, a well-known businessman in New York City, has strong ties to many different industries including the food industry, Wall Street and political sector. He has ties with the Grecos that root back to his childhood, and word in Brooklyn is that he is trying to speed up the release of his former friend and supposed distant cousin, Nicholas Greco, Sr., "the Shark."

JOHN MARINO: I will get on top of that, but first I want to toast to Sapphire Investments being "the King of Wall Street"

BOTH: (*The two toast*) "Saluti to the King of Wall Street."

JOHN MARINO: Changing the subject. I have some exciting news in the healthcare arena. Have you heard of the company Randall Pharmaceuticals?

Charles is getting a text about his afternoon rendezvous with his long-time mistress, Melinda Masters, the location changing to The Plaza Hotel. He looks down at his phone a bit annoyed.

CHARLES MARZIANO: Yes, I'm quite aware, but they are a private company in healthcare.

JOHN MARINO: Yes, and they also are about to launch the first immunotherapy drug for cancer that can be used on kids as well as infants. Their numbers are projected to double in the next two quarters. The kicker is we know one of their board directors and largest shareholder, Pierre Luca. He owns 85%.

CHARLES MARZIANO: Tell me more.

JOHN MARINO: We are in discussions right now. Phillip Delfonte was out with Pierre at Silver Lights a day ago, discussing how we can take their stock public and increase their share value. He is deciding between us and Onyx Equities.

Charles face begins to get extremely red after hearing "Onyx Equities."

CHARLES MARZIANO: Don't get me started about that lousy company. They are pieces of shit and by the time I finish with them, they will be known as Shitty Equities. Whatever you need to do, Marino, even if it's taking a short cut, and covering your tracks this time. You must get Luca's company to go public with us.

When Charles Marziano refers to short cuts, it was his code for doing "dirty work" to make sure they get Pierre's business, so Onyx Equities doesn't stand a chance.

JOHN MARINO: I'm working on it. I do think an introduction between you and Luca next week at the Silver Lights' annual masquerade party could seal the deal.

CHARLES MARZIANO: You know I can't be seen at the titty bars. It will be all over *Page Six.*

JOHN MARINO: I'm good friends with the owners, Tony and Redmond, so privacy is not an issue. The champagne rooms are secure and there is a backdoor entrance. Their anniversary masquerade party would be the perfect time for a meeting with Luca. It's an exclusive, invite-only event for high profile customers, and you can wear a decorative mask.

CHARLES MARZIANO: The mask is a must (*jokingly*). I'm a beast! Look at my face... I look way prettier with that mask. All kidding aside, I can't just go in there with the risk of being recorded with their cameras. If you can assure me with hard evidence that all the video cameras will shut down the night of the ball, I would be open to attending and meeting The Pierre Luca.

John Marino hands out an invitation for the annual masquerade party, with a silver background and grey writing. There are two crystal attachments sparkling near the announcement which says:

SILVER LIGHTS CORDIALLY INVITES YOU TO ITS ANNUAL SEXY MASQUERADE BALL MARCH 12, 2020

SILVER LIGHTS CLUB

Enjoy an Erotic Evening of entertainment, hors d' oeuvre, champagne, and beautiful dancers and guest appearances from celebrities to porn stars

RSVP by MARCH 10, 2020

Text Redmond: 212-000-1112

JOHN MARINO: I will see what I can do to get this meeting going and I will get back to you Monday the 9th. Also, I'm thinking we can reserve the Howard Stern champagne room for the meeting between Luca and the guys.

CHARLES MARZIANO: Now you're talking my language. I heard the Howard Stern champagne room is the closest thing to a soft porn fantasy. (*chuckles*)

JOHN MARINO: You mean hard core fantasy. It will be one for the books.

Charles Marziano is receiving an insane amount of texts from Melinda Masters. She is a high-profile wife of New York Governor Tyler Masters. She is in her mid-forties with looks similar to a modern-day Elizabeth Taylor. She has fair skin, light blue eyes and dark long wavy hair. She has been sleeping with the Beast of Wall Street for years. She is stuck in a cold marriage for politics and money. She met Charles when he was in his mid-forties and just became a big baller on Wall Street. His second marriage was on the rocks, but the affair with Melinda remained strong over the past 14 years, through his two divorces and his fourth marriage. They have kinky sex in five-star hotels and the excitement of sneaking around keeps it going. Both are very careful in taking extra precautions not to get caught. Obviously, Melinda is now texting an urgent enough matter that Charles has to end the meeting.

CHARLES MARZIANO: John, have a good weekend and let me know if you can shut the camera surveillance system down, so I can attend the masquerade ball.

JOHN: I'm on top of it. I had one more matter regarding a smaller company called Vital Pharmaceuticals.

CHARLES MARZIANO: I'm in a rush. We can discuss Monday.

JOHN: OK, before you head out, let's make one more toast for luck and for Sapphire becoming the King of Wall Street.

BOTH: Cheers to The King of Wall Street!

For John to pull off in getting Charles Marziano to attend the ball with no surveillance is no easy task. He has to be clever in his dialogue and strategic in his scenes to ensure all cameras at Silver Lights will be turned off for the biggest meeting of the year.

Will it be a smart move for "the Beast of Wall Street" to attend, knowing he is risking his reputation for a possible Page Six Story that could expose the darkest secrets of Wall Street's finest? How important will it be to have the Beast in attendance at the most important party of the year and how does John find a middle ground with the surveillance situation? He and Redmond will have to come to some compromise to make the big meeting between Pierre Luca, John Marino, and "the Beast of Wall Street" happen.

FADE OUT

Shortly after leaving the office, John Marino made a call to Redmond, letting him know what needed to be done to pull off the attendance of Charles Marziano on the night of the masquerade. Redmond was excited the Beast of Wall Street would be coming, but at the same time, the stress of having to catch the crook associated with the Louis Mazarati scam lessened his excitement.

Redmond was a countryman at heart, with strict values of Christianity and strong ethics, But soon, all that would be washed down the drain in his biggest role yet as detective. He was left to straighten out the dirty mess of money laundering, crooked employees and spotlight the worst villains of Wall Street at the masquerade party.

Just as Redmond was about to call Blake Stevens, financial controller of the Silver Lights enterprise, he remembered he had to call Eddie Maggio to discuss the surveillance options for the night of the ball. As soon as Redmond started to dial, he glanced up to see his girlfriend Barbie on the outside monitor, coming into the club. She was supposed to be at Penthouse right now, working as an undercover dancer. All of sudden, he saw her text, "I'm here to discuss the dirty martini specials. Tony knows I'm heading in."

Redmond hung up the phone before Eddie could answer. Melinda's next two texts were photos captioned "Ron Colombo and Brooks Kennedy outside." The men were photographed outside a limo in what appeared to be a back alley. Redmond couldn't believe what he was seeing. Brooks was dealing with one of the biggest associates from the Marziano family. Why in the hell would Brooks' old money intermingle with the Marzianos' crime money?

The text and photograph triggered something in the countryman's soul from another lifetime. He had a flashback to the 1920s: standing in an alley with Al Capone and a few of his mob associates. Redmond didn't know his exact role in correlation to Capone, but he had a familiar sense of how those drug rings worked, from the time the drugs came off the boats or trucks, smuggled in through the border patrol, and then were sent to the cartel to distribute through the capos and launder through local businesses. The photograph triggered a powerful flashback of his past lifetime as either a mobster or undercover agent, which soon would reveal itself in the storyline of *Hollywood Dreams*.

His rooted values of right and wrong were suddenly kicked to the curb as his animal instincts began to flood over his mind, body, and spirit. Something in the flashback triggered Redmond's personality to shift into a different character, one that was far removed from the countryman's upbringing. He began to see things like a criminal would, in order to catch another criminal. There was no way the countryman was to be made a fool of in the last two acts of *Hollywood Dreams*. He was willing to go to the depths of his former character from the 1920s to take down the crooks behind the money laundering. His heart began to race as he made a call to Brad Rossdale, a top private investigator in New York City who was known to uncover *Page Six* stories. Except this story could possibly end deadly if someone wasn't smart in covering their tracks.

ABOUT THE AUTHOR

 Michelle Lynn is an author, actress, painter, and health founder of The Zen Food Diet (www.zenfoodplan.com). When she is not working on writing, painting, or film projects with The Michelle Lynn Brand, or cooking up her signature health recipes, you can find her traveling to tropical destinations, practicing yoga, dancing, writing, attending health events, and taking long runs along the beach.

She resides in both Austin, Texas and South Florida, and travels regularly to New York City and Los Angeles for on-camera work, acting, writing, fitness modeling, blogging projects, and creative development. She has already published two books in lifestyle and cooking, under The Food Orgy Book Series™. A Tropical Fantasy, A Sensual Guide to Healthy Living and The Chocolate Orgy, A Dating Guide to Cooking up Bittersweet Endings are both are available on Amazon.com

She is working hard on launching a digital campaign for The Silver Lights Book Series this spring 2020 under the website www.silverlightsbooks.com.